"I wish you could tell me what's wrong, Kate,"

Scott said finally.

"It's not important. Really. Just some old trappings hanging on from my youth. Troubles I should have buried long ago. But nothing you can do."

"I don't want to lose your friendship, Kate. I like you too much to have you drift away from me...."

"I'm not drifting. Look, we're standing here talking."

He felt her lie tangled around his heart. Unless God intervened, she was drifting away beyond his grasp like a helium balloon on the wind. An iron fence had risen between them. He could see her and hear her, but he couldn't draw her into his arms. And no matter how firmly he denied his desire, that's exactly where he wanted her to be.

Books by Gail Gaymer Martin

Love Inspired

Upon a Midnight Clear #117
Secrets of the Heart #147

GAIL GAYMER MARTIN

lives in front of her computer in Lathrup Village, Michigan, with her real-life hero, Bob. Growing up in nearby Madison Heights, Gail wrote poems and stories as a child. In her preteens she progressed to Nancy Drew–type mysteries and, in her teen years, to romance where she often killed off her heroine at the dramatic ending. Many years passed before she learned what a "real" romance novel is all about.

Gail is multipublished in nonfiction and fiction, with four novels, two novellas and many more books to come. Besides writing, Gail enjoys singing, public speaking and presenting writers' workshops. She believes that God's gift of humor gets her through even the darkest moment and praises God for his blessings.

She loves to hear from her readers. Write to her at P.O. Box 760063, Lathrup Village, MI, 48076.

Secrets of
the Heart
Gail Gaymer Martin

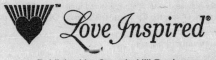

Published by Steeple Hill Books™

STEEPLE HILL BOOKS

Steeple
Hill™

ISBN 0-373-87154-6

SECRETS OF THE HEART

Copyright © 2001 by Gail Gaymer Martin

Visit us at www.steeplehill.com

Printed in U.S.A.

And the secrets of his heart will be laid bare.
—*Corinthians* 14:25

To Jill and Debbie,
who so willingly shared their stories
Thanks to Shelly Thomas at
Lutheran Social Services for her help

Chapter One

Kate Davis jerked her head, pulling her gaze from the delicate anthill growing at the base of the glider swing. With a wry chuckle, she rolled her eyes. "I can't believe I'm sitting here watching ants have more fun than I am."

Though the old oak offered her shade, the May sun sneaked beneath the tree branches and warmed her arms. She stretched her legs in front of her and scanned the backyard, admiring the veil of purple blossoms weighting the lilac trees and filling the air with a rich, sweet scent. This year spring came late to Michigan, and a small bed of mixed tulips added a splash of color in the morning sunlight.

Everything was bright and cheery, except Kate. Spring meant new birth, a new surprise every day, but her life seemed to drag on with endless mediocrity. She'd spent the past hour comparing her rather boring personal life with her overly impassioned career and wished her days lay somewhere in the middle of those two emotions.

A lazy Saturday afternoon wasn't too bad, but those long, empty evenings were another story. She sat too many nights in front of the television or played board games with her housemate, Phyllis Ryan.

Wondering about this particular Saturday, Kate noticed again the column of industrious ants. As a row paraded over the sand and into the hole, another army marched back out. At least the ants were doing something. Kate pushed herself up from the swing. Enough of this, she thought as she strode across the grass and headed for the back door. I refuse to spend another minute mesmerized by insects. Something had to change. She needed a plan.

"Phyllis," she called, stepping into the back hall. "Let's do some—"

A piercing shriek shot from the front of the house. With her heart hammering, Kate dashed to the kitchen doorway and barreled toward her friend's heartrending screech.

Stumbling into the living room, Kate froze, witnessing her housemate clutched in a powerful set of arms with her feet flailing above the carpet at the open front door.

Kate grabbed the first thing she laid her hands on and Kate darted toward them, raising the weapon over her head. "Take your hands off her," she shouted.

Kate's last word was jumbled in Phyllis's hysterical cries of "No."

Phyllis bolted from the man's arms, panic covering her face, and raised her hand in protection. "Kate, no, this is my brother, Scott."

Her cheeks on fire, Kate gaped at the two startled faces and lowered the flowered umbrella. "I'm sorry, Phyllis." Kate's look darted from her friend to the widened nutmeg-brown eyes of her dazed brother, then to her pitiful weapon and back to Phyllis. "I had no idea you were expecting anyone. I heard the scream and—"

"It's okay, Kate. I wasn't expecting him, either." Phyllis turned her head to peer good-naturedly at the square, solid male at her side. "Was I?"

"No," he said with a chuckle, "I wanted to surprise you. But I was the one surprised." He eyed Kate. "You could have fractured my skull with that pretty umbrella."

Kate scrutinized the pathetic weapon and offered a halfhearted grin, adding, "I'm sorry." But, inwardly, she cringed with embarrassment, thinking that at thirty-four she should have better sense than to attack without knowing the situation.

With the two still gawking, Kate edged backward and slid the umbrella into the stand. When she looked up and caught his gaze, an unwelcome, unpleasant memory of her adolescence inched into her thoughts. "Please," she said, "come in…while I silently vanish into the sunset."

"Don't you dare," Phyllis said. "I want you and Scott to get to know each other."

Phyllis wrapped her arm around her brother's waist. "It's been too long, hasn't it?"

"More than a year, I think" he said.

"How about something to drink? And maybe a sandwich?" Phyllis beckoned him toward the kitchen.

Scott gave Kate a fleeting grin as he passed and followed his sister.

Addled, Kate held back, struggling with her reaction to the strapping man. With one lengthy look, she had flown back in time. Back to high school. Back to her nonexistent confidence and her naive desires.

What had caused her to sink into an abyss of miserable memories? The answer hit her before the question left her mind. Scott's build. Not his near six-foot stature, but his broad, square frame like a football player. Thick neck, powerful chest, strong muscular legs, and the bulging arms she saw wrapped around Phyllis. She cringed with a painful recollection.

"Kate?" Phyllis's voice sailed through the archway, and Kate pushed away the nagging, guilt-ridden memories and planted a pleasant expression on her face. Straightening her shoulders, she strolled into the kitchen.

"You're not embarrassed, are you?" Scott asked, his voice brimming with amusement.

"Nothing I can't handle," Kate said, sinking into an adjacent chair at the table.

"I commend you for protecting my baby sister."

She gave him a feeble grin. "I doubt if an umbrella could've done much damage."

Without comment, he leaned against the chair back and chuckled.

Putting an end to their silly conversation, Kate eyed Phyllis at the counter. "Can I help?"

"No, you two talk while I make up some tuna salad." She turned toward them. "Does that sound good?"

With their agreeable nods, Phyllis returned to her task.

Avoiding Scott's scrutiny, Kate lifted the pitcher and poured a tumbler of lemonade. "So, what brings you to town?" she asked, focusing on the condensation forming on her glass. With the first sip, her cheeks puckered at the zesty, tart tang that rolled on her tongue.

"I'm doing my residency at County General."

"Residency?" She hesitated, then remembered. "Ah, Phyl mentioned you're a doctor." Her finger traced the rim of the glass. "What's your speciality?"

He shook his head. "General practice."

Surprised by his response, she straightened in the chair. "No specialty, that's rare."

"Threw you a curve?" he said. "Financially, I could earn more as a specialist, but I like the idea of family practice."

She liked what he said, and a warm feeling settled over her. Kate leaned back, studying his animated, handsome face. "That's nice. Family practice seems to be vanishing, but specialists are too costly for young families. Especially single parents."

Seeing a scowl dart across his face, curiosity needled Kate. "Did I say something wrong?" she asked.

"No, I, ah, well, you're not a single parent, are you?"

His question left Kate with an uneasy feeling. "What would make you ask that?"

He shrugged. "I don't know. You sounded serious."

"It's a serious problem."

He nodded, and they sat in silence. Kate wished she'd not interjected her ever serious concerns. He was fun and lighthearted, and she'd put a weight on the conversation.

Phyllis slid them each a tuna sandwich, garnished with lettuce and a dill pickle spear. "Pretty fancy," she said cutting the heavy silence that had risen between them. She settled into a chair. "Don't let Kate fool you. She's not always this serious."

Scott hesitated, as if waiting for her to respond.

Kate's mind went blank, unable to think of anything to say. For a moment, her thoughts were tangled in the past and the present, unsorted and unwelcome.

"Kate works with me," Phyllis said, "at Children's Haven."

Kate could have hugged her for covering her growing discomfort.

"Ahh, that explains your comment, then," Scott said, relaxing against the chair. "So, what do you do there?"

Hating to be the center of attention, Kate felt pinned by his gaze. "I'm a social worker."

"Then I can see what you mean. Lots of tension, I imagine. Innocent children hurt by troubled parents."

Kate nodded. "Some, but often it's just a sad situation that time can heal. The problems vary."

"Last year when I was an intern, I ran into all kinds of problems. My skin crawls when I remember some of the abused kids we treated." He blew a stream of air from his lungs.

"Let's talk about something more pleasant," Kate suggested, hoping to turn the attention to someone else.

His scowl faded, replaced by a smile. "Okay, let's talk about you…away from Children's Haven."

Noting her failed attempt, Kate's stomach sank. She shook her head. "I said pleasant, not pitiful." She sent him another halfhearted grin.

"Oh, don't be modest," Phyllis inserted. "Kate does all kinds of wonderful things. When I lost my roommate, she offered to share this house with me. She didn't even know me that well."

"I did, too. Anyway, it helps with expenses. It's worked out great." Determined to change the subject, she picked up her untouched sandwich. "Isn't anyone going to eat?"

They complied, and for a few minutes, they concentrated on lunch. When the conversation returned, Scott and Phyllis chatted about his internship experiences and their family.

Kate contemplated their easy rapport. She envied what seemed to be a real friendship. Her only sibling, Kristin, and she were as different as country music and opera...and about as conflicting. Kate had never known that kind of relationship with her sister.

Feeling a little like an eavesdropper, Kate listened to their reunion for a while. But after finishing her sandwich, she drained her glass and carried the dishes to the sink.

When the conversation lulled, Kate prepared her escape. "I have some things to do so I'll let you two reminisce." She jutted her hand toward Scott's. "Nice to meet you."

He captured her fingers with his massive hand.

Fighting not to recoil, Kate felt swallowed in his grasp.

"Don't hide because of me," he said. "When you finish, come back."

She nodded, knowing she wouldn't, and fled for the safety of her room.

Closing the door, a sigh rattled from her chest. She hated envy. And watching Phyllis and her brother filled her with it.

One thing she learned in Sunday school was coveting is a sin. Still, she'd spent her youth yearning to be her older sister. Kristin seemed perfect, while much of Kate's life centered around her transgressions, especially in her parents' eyes.

She sat on her bed and folded her hands in her lap. Why did she allow herself to sink into a state of self-pity when she talked with Scott? Instead of enjoying the conversation, she spent the time trying to block the memories he aroused.

He'd been amiable and warm. She recalled his teasing eyes and generous smile—and his huge dimples. She pictured the deep indentations in his cheeks when he gave her an amused look.

Imagining Scott as a physician settled in her mind. His sincere face would soothe a mother's concern, and his boyish charm would appeal to children. He'd make a good family doctor.

Falling back against the mattress, Kate closed her eyes. What kind of face did she have? Worried? Serious? No, she laughed when situations were comical. But…sometimes, things didn't seem funny to her. Maybe, the problem was her occupation, as Phyllis had suggested. Sad, depressing situations and frightened, rejected children.

No matter, she tried to act positive. That was one thing for which she prided herself. Thinking back to her youthful mistakes—she added a capital *M* to the word—she'd made the best of her senseless, shameful offense. She thanked God for lifting her from depression and guiding her to a purposeful career. Social work was the best part of her life.

Interrupting her musing, a tap sounded against her bedroom door. She noted the comfortable, safe barricade and, against her will, slid from the bed. When she turned the knob, Phyllis pushed open the door without waiting.

"Not feeling well?" Phyllis asked, her brows knit with concern.

"Resting. I'm lazy today." Kate distorted the truth to cover her wavering emotions.

"Then you'll like our plan. Scott wants to take us to dinner. What do you say? And he said no's not a choice."

The invitation made her grin, but apprehension nipped at her. "Okay," Kate said, praying she could view Scott with clearer eyes.

"Great," Phyllis said, then added in a whisper, "and I hope you don't mind I invited him to spend the night in the guest room. That way I can get him to go to church with us tomorrow. He's a natural sloth on Sunday mornings."

Her eager eyes searched Kate's, and she couldn't disappoint her friend. Anyway, the house seemed as much Phyllis's as hers.

"Sure," Kate said, hoping she sounded sincere.

Sitting together in a restaurant booth, Scott observed Kate throughout dinner. Though she seemed amiable, he sensed she was uncomfortable, and he wished he could help her relax.

Kate stared at her half-full plate. Direct eye contact seemed to fluster her. Scott had tried to keep from making direct contact, but he couldn't stop himself. Her eyes were captivating—a soft, misty brown with flecks of green and yellow. Hazel, he guessed.

Shifting his focus, he admired her sun-streaked hair hanging straight and shoulder length with a part to one side. Occasionally, she lifted her fingers and pushed the loose strands from her forehead. She was a beautiful woman. Admiring her aroused many questions. For one, why wasn't she married or, at least, going with someone?

"So what are you planning to do with yourself, Scott?" Phyllis asked. "I mean other than your residency."

"First thing, I need an apartment. Mom offered my old room, but that seemed too…adolescent." He grinned. "I'll find someone to share expenses. Like the two of you are doing. Once I have my own practice, I'll buy a house."

"I feel smothered in an apartment," Kate said. "No fresh air, except a window or one of those tiny balconies. A house gives you lots of room for privacy…or companionship, if you want it."

"A house would be nice," Scott agreed.

Silence fell over them, and he peered at his sister, then at Kate who again averted her eyes. Knowing Phyllis, he could almost hear the wheels turning. In a moment, she'd have some kind of plan. If he were a betting man, he'd make a secure wager.

His sister's pensive face edged upward, then a smile crept to her lips. "I've got it."

Hearing Phyllis's excited voice, Kate's attention left her plate.

"Why not stay with us?" Phyllis said. "Pay rent until you find a place?" She pivoted from him to Kate's astonished expression. "What do you say?" she asked.

Kate seemed to shrink into her seat. Obviously, she hated the idea.

"No, I can't do that," he said, hoping to smooth the tension. "Too much like living with Mom and Dad."

"It is not," Phyllis said. "We're nearly the same age. Thirty-two and twenty-nine. We're contemporaries." She flashed them a bright grin. "So what do you say?"

"I might be your brother, Phyllis, but the house belongs to Kate, too." He hoped his sister would catch on and back off.

"She won't mind, will you?" She turned to Kate whose expression flickered from startled to defeated.

Kate faltered. "If, ah, that works for you, Scott, we can manage…I mean, we can work things out. It's only temporary."

He studied her, wondering why she was agreeing to a plan she obviously despised. He knew the answer without asking. She was plain old nice. Truly compassionate. It went with her job.

"Okay, then," Phyllis said, grasping his arm. "You're our new roomie. I think the guest room will work fine. You and I will share the bathroom up-stairs. Kate's bedroom and bath are on the first floor.''

Kate had agreed, but the plan was obviously putting her out. From her expression, Scott figured he'd be smart to start apartment hunting tomorrow morning…right after church. *Church.* Somehow, he'd conceded to go there, too.

The next day, Kate ignored the anthill and leaned back in the glider. She felt more optimistic. Maybe things would work out after all. The worship service that morning had lifted her spirits, and though Scott taunted Phyllis about making him go to church, he'd been a good sport. At first, he stumbled through a couple of melodies, but many of the hymns he sang out in a confident baritone voice that she had to admit was pretty good.

On the way home, they sang one of the morning's hymns at the top of their lungs. The words lingered in her head. Yes, they'll know we are Christians by our love. The experience felt nice. Like family.

A scowl edged across her face and she pushed it aside. No room for self-pity. She wanted to enjoy the rest of the day before she returned to work tomorrow.

A shadow feel across her legs, and Kate snapped her head upward. She found herself gazing into a pair of mischievous eyes that sent her heart pitching like a rowboat in a storm.

''You look too relaxed,'' Scott said, dropping

down beside her on the glider. "Thought I'd bug you a little. Plus I can use some rays."

He shifted on the seat, stretched out his legs, and lifted his nose in the air. "What's that wonderful smell? You?"

His bluntness made her laugh. "I should say yes, but it's probably the lilacs."

He scanned one side of the yard, then the other. "I suppose you're right. There's sure a lot of them." He leaned toward her and sniffed. "But you smell pretty sweet yourself."

"Thanks." His innocent frankness amazed her.

"Silliness aside, Kate, I really want to thank you for letting me stay here. I promise I'll find an apartment soon. I know that you weren't thrilled—"

She squirmed against the seat, mortified that her feelings had been so open. "I didn't mean to be unkind. To be honest, all I could think of was confusion with the three of us trying to share the house, but I've had time to let the idea settle in." She noted his serious eyes. "It's fine. Really."

"Well, I appreciate your generosity. My folks are great, but living at home when I've been away so long—"

Kate touched his arm. "You don't have to explain that to me. I'd feel exactly like you do. Maybe more so." The tense teen years filled her mind. "You're welcome to stay until you find someplace you really like."

"That's a deal," he said, reaching toward her for a handshake.

She grinned at his amiable gesture and tucked her smaller palm against his. His smile and the feel of his large, warm hand pressing against her skin radiated up her arm. Heat rose to her cheeks. She felt foolish. Why did she flush at his touch?

Scott released her hand and relaxed against the glider. "I'm not looking forward to the next few days."

"No?" His comment aroused her curiosity. "Why?"

"Nothing, really. Tomorrow I start work. Every hospital has its own idiosyncrasies. Its own hierarchy. You know how it is."

Thinking of her own situation, she nodded. Now, she felt at home at the Haven, but her first months there were filled with uncertainty while she learned the rules and protocol. Only the laws remained the same.

"I don't know what I'll be doing yet. Except rotating floors," he added.

"Dr. Barlow's a resident at County General, and he has hours at Children's Haven. He does physicals on the intakes and handles the usual cases of measles, colds and head lice."

"Head lice. Thanks." He raised his arms and stretched them across the back of the glider. "For a while, I'll be doing all the dirty work that the practicing physicians don't want to do." He shot her an apologetic grin. "Sorry, I sound like a prima donna."

"No, you don't," she said.

Amazed, Kate stretched her legs into the sun and leaned back. She felt relaxed sitting beside a man with no expectations, no come-ons, no false flattery. Despite her qualms, Scott gave her interesting conversation and good honest fun. She might enjoy having a real male friend.

Chapter Two

A wooden chair scraped against the bare floor, and Kate leaned back, studying the angry ten-year-old who was scowling in front of her desk.

"Then if you don't want to talk, Eddie, I'll have to see you again on Thursday."

"An' I won't talk then, either," he declared.

With his fists knotted, the boy spun around and charged toward the exit like a freight train. But as he approached the doorway, Phyllis stepped into Kate's office and did a quick two-step to avoid being run over.

Eddie shot through the doorway without looking back.

"What was that all about?" Phyllis asked.

"Eddie's in a bad mood today. Glad he didn't run you over."

Phyllis's halfhearted smile echoed Kate's feelings. She dealt with too many angry children wanting to punch their way out of every situation.

"So what's up?" Kate noticed the manila file folder and assumed Phyllis hadn't dropped by to visit.

"A new six-year-old girl arrived today. You may want to work her into your schedule tomorrow." She dropped the file on Kate's desk. "Amber's really timid and having a hard time."

"Why is she here?"

"She lives with her grandma, but her grandma's in the hospital. There's no one else. That's all I know."

"Sad." Kate shook her head. "When you get back tell the housemother to bring her down. I'll see her now."

Phyllis squeezed Kate's forearm. "Great. I figured you would."

Kate shook her head. "You're getting to know me too well."

An uneasy expression rose on Phyllis's face, and she paused. "Ah, speaking of that, I've been wanting to ask you. Are you okay with Scott at the house? After I invited him, I realized I should have asked you first. In private."

"It's fine, Phyl. It's temporary, and he's been very considerate." Discomfort threaded through her, remembering her first unhappy reaction.

"Whew! I'm relieved." Phyllis blew a stream of air from between her pursed lips. "Scott nailed me to the wall the other day, saying I had overstepped our friendship."

"It's temporary. And it's been fun." She tried to picture Scott angry at Phyllis, but couldn't. Jolts of envy pricked her conscience. "You two have such a great relationship. Honest and…sort of, looking out for each other."

"We do," Phyllis said, her voice growing tender.

"I never had that kind of relationship with my sister," Kate admitted, then wished she hadn't. Talking about her association with Kristin was too difficult.

"No? That's too bad. Scott's been a really great big brother."

"I can see that," Kate said, fingering the file on her desk.

Phyllis backed toward the doorway. "See you at lunch."

"Don't forget to send Amber down," Kate reminded her.

"I'll have Denise bring her here right away."

Kate nodded, pushing their conversation out of her mind. She opened the child's folder, then thumbed through the pages, searching for a relative, but found none. Only the ailing grandmother.

Closing the folder, Kate rose and wandered to the window, longing to be outside under the powder-blue sky. Unbidden, her thoughts turned to Scott. Living with them for the past five days, he'd been considerate and kindhearted. Since he began work, Scott spent his days at the hospital. When he arrived home, they had dinner together, then he vanished. He seemed to respect her privacy.

At times, Kate wished he didn't. When he exited the room, loneliness filled the space he'd left empty. Until last Saturday, the house had never rung with so much good cheer and laughter.

Yet, once in a while when she looked at Scott a certain way, the old sorrow rose in her—sorrow she presumed she had overcome long ago. His sturdy body was so much like her memory of Ron from her teens. Kate bit her bottom lip, wishing she would stop comparing. Forget Ron. She'd learned from her terrible experience and directed her energy toward doing good for others...even though she'd not done right by herself.

A firm rap on the doorjamb snapped Kate to attention. The housemother leaned into the room, prodding a tiny blond child through the doorway.

"Here's Amber," the woman said.

"Thanks, Denise." Kate stepped toward the child.

Denise nodded and vanished around the corner.

Confusion and fright etched the girl's pale face, and she stared at Kate with wide eyes.

"Amber, I'm Kate. Would you sit with me, please?" She beckoned the child toward the chair.

The girl froze just inside the doorway, glancing behind her for the housemother, then looking back at Kate with helplessness.

Kate ambled toward the door, praying the girl wouldn't bolt in fear like a startled fawn. She rested her hand on the child's back and guided her to a seat.

Instead of sitting behind her desk, Kate grasped a stuffed toy lamb from a nearby shelf and joined the child in a second chair.

Amber focused on the stuffed, curly-haired animal.

As a diversion, Kate petted the toy while she distracted the child with quiet conversation. When she sensed Amber had relaxed, she placed the stuffed animal in the girl's lap and began in earnest.

"Tell me about your grandmother."

Amber's gaze clung to the lamb. "She's sick."

"I know. I'm sorry." She studied the sorrowful child. "What happened?"

"She wouldn't wake up," Amber murmured.

Kate leaned forward and spoke tenderly. "I bet you were frightened."

Amber nodded.

"What did you do?" Kate asked.

"I called 911 like Grandma taught me."

From the report, Kate recalled the woman had a stroke. "You were very brave."

Her eyes widened. "I was?"

"Yes, you were very smart to call for help." Kate hesitated with her next question, then plowed ahead. "Where are your mother and father, Amber?"

The child's upturned gaze swept the room, then she shrugged.

"You don't know?" Kate asked.

Lowering her eyes, Amber shook her head.

"Has it been a long time since you've seen them?"

A deep scowl worked across the child's face.

Kate waited. Then, she tried a different tack. "Did you see your parents at Christmas?"

"No." She responded without delay.

Kate searched for a new approach. "When's your birthday, Amber?"

"March 19."

"Did you see your mother or father then?" Kate asked.

"I don't have a mother or father."

Caught off guard, Kate swallowed her startled gasp. "Did they die?"

Amber shrugged again. "I don't know."

Kate slumped against the chair. Amber's resemblance to Kate as a child was uncanny. Kate searched the girl's face. Though she knew better, Amber, with her fair skin and blond curls—especially her hazel eyes—could have been Kate's own child. She pushed away the longing.

What a heavy burden, Lord, to place on such tiny shoulders. Kate's sorrowful past rose again in her appreciation...contemplating where her daughter was now.

"Okay, here's my deal."

Hearing, Scott's voice, Kate spun away from the television. An unexpected sensation rippled up her arms, and she ran her hand down its length to erase the feeling.

He dropped beside her on the sofa. "I need a woman's opinion on this apartment thing. I've found a couple in the paper that sound interesting."

She looked toward him for the want ads, but he was empty-handed. "Well, let me see the paper," she said.

Dimples appeared with his amused grin. "No, I mean *look* at the apartments. I can read the ads by myself."

Taming her confusion, Kate sorted her thoughts. "Did you ask Phyllis?"

His smile faded. "She's busy Saturday. So how about you—"

"I'm busy, too. Sorry."

"Oh." His voice sagged as quickly as his face.

She'd never seen him so disappointed, like a kid who's been told he can't have a puppy. Feeling the need to explain, she added, "Phyllis and I are both involved with HELP this weekend."

A quizzical expression replaced the frown. "What's help?"

"It's an acronym for Helping the Elderly Live Proudly. A group of us from the church do whatever needs to be done for the senior citizens in the community. Yard work or painting walls. Grocery shopping."

"You're kidding?"

"No." She weighed what he meant. "Sometimes we just visit and listen to their stories. A lot of them live alone and love for someone to stop by just to say hi."

"Now there's something I can do."

"You think we're silly?" Kate asked.

Scott studied her concerned face and wanted to laugh, but he'd already hurt her feelings. "I'm only teasing you."

Her shoulders relaxed, then shifted toward him on the sofa. "You think it's a good idea?"

"Sure." He really couldn't understand how one person wanted to give so much to others. "You're just full of surprises, aren't you? I'd think you'd be tired of worrying about people after you work all day. Isn't that enough?"

"No, I enjoy it. It's what Christians are supposed to do." She pushed a few strands of hair behind her ear.

"You make me feel guilty. I'm not that compassionate."

Her face softened, and she touched his arm. "I saw you at church when that little toddler used your leg for a prop. Your whole face lit up when you knelt down and talked to him. You'll make a great family doctor."

Her candid comment was refreshing. He slipped his arm around her shoulders and gave her a playful hug. "Thanks, you're too generous."

To his surprise, a soft pink flush rose to her cheeks. Watching her smile fade, he discretely slid his arm to the back of the sofa. "So, getting back to my dilemma, I honestly don't want to apartment hunt alone. I'll rent something, and when it's too late, I'll realize it doesn't have closets. Or a shower.''

Her face brightened at his silly chatter and he wanted to hug her again. Yet, he faltered, perplexed as to where his mind was headed. He reined his errant thoughts and focused on Kate's pensive face.

''We could go later in the afternoon,'' she said. ''We usually finish early. By one or so. Is that too late?''

''Not at all.'' A sense of excitement shivered up his back, and he wondered if it were the thought of getting a place of his own…or just being with Kate. ''What if I go with you Saturday? Maybe you'll get done faster.''

He expected to see her smile again, but she didn't.

Saturday morning Scott slipped into old jeans and a T-shirt. At the bottom of the stairs, noise drifted from the kitchen along with the smell of coffee. When he entered, the two women were peering into cardboard boxes.

''What's up?'' he asked.

Like marionette's on strings, they jumped and swung around, clutching their chests.

''Could you make a little more noise when you sneak up on us?'' Phyllis asked.

''Next time, I'll whistle,'' he said, ambling toward them. ''What's in the boxes?''

''Stuff,'' Kate said. ''Have some coffee and toast if you want, because we need to get going.''

He stepped to their sides, resting a hand on each

one's shoulder and peered between them into the boxes. "Let's see what you've got in there."

Kate moved from under his grasp, grabbed a mug from the hook, and set it in his unoccupied hand. "There. Now, drink first, then you can tote."

He arched a brow and marched to the toaster. After he dropped in the bread, Scott leaned against the counter and waited. He enjoyed watching the women bustle around the kitchen, packing what he guessed was a lunch basket. Being honest with himself, Scott knew it was Kate he watched.

Periodically, she paused and pushed stray hair from her cheek, tucking it behind her ear. Her face looked rested and glowed with sleep—or maybe the excitement of taking care of people. She amazed him.

"Why are you staring at me?" Kate asked, her face shifting from quizzical to suspicious.

As he raised his hands in the air like a captured criminal, the toaster popped, and the sound triggered his imagination. He clutched his chest, spiraled as if shot, and grabbed the counter as he sank to the floor. "Tell my wife I loved her," he said in halting words. He jerked two fabricated spasms before his final dramatic death.

When he peeked with one eye, Phyllis and Kate stood over him, shaking their heads like he was an idiot.

"Looks like you're ready to carry out the cartons," Phyllis said

Embarrassed at his ridiculous, unappreciated

drama, he gave them a haughty look, then rose, wiped off his hands on his denim-clad legs and eyed them.

"I haven't had my toast yet," he said.

"Less drama, more food," Phyllis said shooting him a grin.

Feeling foolish, he buttered his toast in silence and wolfed it down with a few swigs of coffee before the two women's toes tapping, let him know it was time to leave.

"So, what can I do for you?" he asked, knowing before he spoke.

"Help us with those boxes. Or are you too weak from loss of blood?" Kate asked, flashing him a smirky smile.

He ignored her, walked to the counter and peeked into two hefty, cardboard boxes, containing spray bottles, buckets, newspaper, sponges and squeegees. He peered at Kate over his shoulder. "I hope this isn't lunch."

She shook her head. "Lunch is in the wicker basket. Pastor Ray called last night. We're washing windows."

He hoisted a box to his chest and headed for the car. When he returned, Scott grabbed the last box, and on his final trip to his car, Kate held the door for him.

As he passed, a whiff of her sweet fruity fragrance filled his senses. Outdoors, he drew in a deep breath to rid his heady thoughts. Phyllis followed on his heels with the food basket, and finally, Kate, lugging a gallon container and locking the door.

Scott stood by the trunk, his mind whirring again at what he'd gotten himself into. Spending the afternoon with a group of church people and lonely senior citizens wasn't quite what he had in mind as a relaxing day off with Kate. But if the afternoon didn't thrill him, Kate did. He found her intriguing. A real paradox of a woman.

In the church parking lot, Kate stood beside Scott's broad frame, caught again in the memories that hauled her back to high school. Shamefully, she recalled her pride when she stood at Ron's side, praying her sister would pass by and see her with one of the popular football players.

When she introduced Scott to her friends, she sensed he was distracted despite his handshake and pleasant expression. Once in a while, she detected him staring at her, and a wave of self-consciousness washed over her.

While she talked with one of the workers, Scott meandered toward the car. After the woman left, Kate watched him, her curiosity growing. Finally, she headed his way. He had his head tucked beneath the trunk lid, puttering with the cartons.

"What are you doing?"

He lifted his head with a guilty grin. "Nothing."

Kate gave him a poke. "You're into the food basket." The words burst from her when she saw cookie crumbs clinging to his bottom lip. "That's lunch."

"Don't I get some pay for following you around like you're the, uh, Prodigal Son?"

Laughter bubbled up from Kate's chest. "Prodigal Son? I think you mean the Good Samaritan." Kate said, playfully arching an eyebrow.

Scott shrugged. "I knew it was one of those stories."

"Did I hear you say you're a Good Samaritan?" Pastor Ray asked, as he joined them. "That's what HELP needs. More Good Samaritans." He extended his arm toward Scott.

"Scott Ryan," he said, grasping his hand. "Kate's friend."

Kate peered at Scott. "And Phyllis's brother and he's *Dr.* Scott Ryan."

"Doctor? Nice of you to join us," the clergy said as they shook hands. "Everyone's appreciated."

He handed Kate a slip of paper. "Your group is washing windows at the three homes on the list. Oh, and you'll put up their screens if they're not hung already." He pivoted, surveying the crowd in the parking lot. "Who are we missing?" he asked as he ambled toward the next group.

"Ready?" Phyllis asked.

Scott shrugged, "I guess."

"I'll get Darren." Phyllis pointed behind her and darted away.

"She has her eye on him," Kate said, watching

her flit across the asphalt. "The poor man doesn't have a chance."

Scott turned to watch them. "Doesn't look like he wants one."

Kate studied Phyllis walking arm in arm with Darren, and a sense of envy rifled through her. She cringed inwardly at the familiar feeling. One of these days Phyllis and Darren would be a happy twosome. And Kate would…live alone.

She rode with Scott while Darren's truck followed with two ladders and Phyllis. A few streets from the church, Kate motioned Scott to slow down. "Here," she said, pointing to a small bungalow in desperate need of paint.

Within minutes, the equipment was assembled on the grass, and Kate knocked on the door.

Scott stayed by the car, watching Kate and questioning his growing fondness. As time passed, a pleasant feeling wove through him, a warm, cozy glow. He'd spent too long with his nose to the proverbial grindstone, buried in textbooks while he learned to diagnose diseases and procedures to treat them.

Moving in with his sister and Kate, even temporarily, helped him return to the real world of fun, family…and friendships. That's what he'd really missed for so long. An old ache cut at his heart when he thought back. He'd pushed all the nagging desires into the "contamination bin" where they belonged. Why did the old wound open again?

Scott reined his negative thoughts and pushed the

pleasant moment back into focus. Watching Kate waiting at the door, he admired her figure. In pale-rose slacks and a pink-and-white T-shirt, she looked as delicate and wispy as spun sugar. Probably as sweet, he calculated, seeing her cheerful greeting when a gaunt gray-haired lady answered the door.

The elderly woman clung to the doorjamb with one hand while the other gripped the screen like a crutch. His medical knowledge needled his curiosity, and he edged forward for clearer observation. The woman squinted into the sunlight, her eyes pale and glazed. To diagnose the situation, he needed to talk with her.

With a final pat of the senior's arm, Kate bounced from the porch ready to work and beckoned them toward her.

Scott tucked away his worries for a more appropriate time. He filled the buckets from the outdoor hose, and they attacked the windows—and at times themselves—as they sloshed and dripped their way around the house.

The sun rose in the sky, and heat shimmered off the cement driveway. Scott studied Kate as she descended the ladder, watching a tiny rivulet of perspiration roll down her cheek. He grasped a clean rag and wet it at the tap.

When she stepped to the ground, Scott met her with a moist cloth, pressing it against her cheek.

She jumped at first, then smiled and mopped her face. "Feels good," she said. "See." She drew the damp rag along his neckline.

"You can nurse me to health, anytime," he said, pivoting around to face her. When he looked into her gentle eyes, his breath caught in his throat. Colors like burnished leaves watched him from beneath a shapely brow. Her high, full cheekbones were tinted by the sun, and a few delicate freckles dappled her cute turned-up nose.

Unmoving, Kate searched his face, a puzzled look growing in her eyes.

Lifting his thumb and finger, he tilted her chin, longing to kiss her perfect full lips. She looked real and honest. "You okay?" he asked, grasping for something sensible to say.

"Fine. And you?" Her words were as inane and senseless as his.

Kate's smile sent a warm charge down his spine. He chuckled and dropped his hand, wishing he could feel like this all the time instead of being buried under a pile of medical journals. Kate brought out the best in him—silliness, yes, but also a delight for living instead of only doctoring. He liked that, and he had to remember the difference.

With thoughtful silence, they shifted back to the wet cloths, spray bottles and the fleeting time.

"We'd better finish," Scott said. "We have two more to go, and I'm already hungry."

She chuckled and bent down to gather the equipment.

Hungry? Scott closed his eyes. Yes, he was starving, but for more than food. He'd allow a college relationship to kill his taste for courtship. But the right woman could make him feel complete and whole and loved. When he lifted his lids, Kate's delicate frame filled his eyes.

relationship would her work for Scott's help for the next winters, remember... from their completed and year-after-loved. When he tried his talk, knew someone must either because

Chapter Three

Kate leaned against the chair and relaxed the tension that knotted between her shoulder blades. She ached from the stretching and climbing during their window-washing marathon. Otherwise, the morning had been enjoyable. Scott's presence made the job easy, and the time flew by. As always, he added a little humor and a few shining moments to her usually mundane life.

But the afternoon was different. The apartment search had been useless to the point of ridiculous. Scott clowned through the buildings, evading his rising disappointment. Now, allowing his emotions to surface, he sat at the kitchen table, a disheartened expression on his face.

Kate rose and gathered plates from the kitchen table, sensing she needed to say something. "I know you're disappointed. The apartments sure sounded better in the paper than in person."

"I should've been prepared. Things don't always work the way we like."

"Think positive," Kate said.

Scott shot her a glance. "Okay, Miss Optimistic, make me smile."

When she thought of the cramped, unkempt places they'd visited, discouragement was logical, but for Kate, hope sprung eternal. "Don't forget. There's always next week. And we're not kicking you out of here, yet."

"I'm grateful." Though she'd made him grin, his expression slid immediately to discouragement.

Kate turned back to the sink. "Maybe Phyllis will go with you next week. She might have a more discerning eye."

Kate said the words, though the idea didn't set well. She had enjoyed their time together. Even though teasing and laughing at the ugly apartments were a cover-up, the camaraderie felt fresh and exciting.

"You mean you're willing to miss another adventurous apartment-hunting experience?" He flashed her a facetious grin, but his face grew tender. "You look tired."

"Just a little. But I enjoyed the day. And the company was nice," she added after a moment struggling with whether she should say what she felt.

"Thanks," he said, rising. "The feeling is mutual."

He rooted his hand on her shoulder, sending a charge down her arm.

"Mind if I rummage through the CDs?" he asked.

"Rummage away," she said, trying to rein in the sweep of emotion that mystified her. Was her mind playing games with Scott? Or was their friendship taking on a new edge?

For so many years, she'd pushed amorous thoughts from her mind. She had built a wall whenever she sensed a man was interested in her. Relationships were too complicated. They required honesty, and she wasn't ready to spill out her past.

Besides, her life wasn't useless or unbearable. She was a good social worker. Her work gave her purpose. She'd decided long ago to let her career be her focus, even though sometimes her personal life seemed too lonely. And too empty.

But she's made her bed, and now—as her mother had so aptly put it—she would lie in it…alone.

As a young teen, she'd longed to be an adult, assuming things would be better, believing that wisdom and charm would suddenly wash over her and all her feelings of worthlessness would go away.

But it didn't happen that way. Instead, she realized that the sins of the past press on a person's soul. She'd lost all thoughts of a husband or family.

"Nice jazz discs."

Kate turned her head toward the doorway. "Thanks, it's good thinking music."

He nodded, leaning against the doorjamb. "Can I help?"

"No, this is it." She slid the last glass into the washer. "How about some coffee? Or tea?"

"Either's fine."

Within minutes, they entered the living room with soft, melodic jazz filling the air and their mugs emitting the rich fragrance of Darjeeling tea.

"Nothing could be nicer," Scott said, easing into a chair cushion.

But, sinking into the sofa, Kate thought differently. The mood would be more pleasant if she could tell him all the things that bothered her. She couldn't. She pressed her shoulders against the cushion to relax.

The music wove through their genial conversation until Scott's concerned expression met hers.

"Did I say something wrong?" Kate asked.

"No, why?"

"You look worried."

He gave her a halfhearted grin. "My face doesn't hide much, does it?"

"What's wrong?" she asked, her curiosity more than aroused.

"I've been thinking all day about the lady whose windows we washed," he said.

"Which lady?"

"The first house. I don't know her name."

"Mrs. Finkell. Why?"

"She's not well. Did you notice how she clung to the door to steady herself? She's really weak."

"Scott, she's old. She's pushing ninety, I think."

"It's more than age, Kate. I need to talk with her."

"We can't interfere with the seniors' lives. We wash windows and rake leaves," Kate said.

"And talk, you told me." Scott leaned forward with his elbows propped on his knees and folded his hands. "I'm a doctor, Kate. I can't help but notice symptoms. We could drop by for a visit sometime, couldn't we?"

"Sure, on the Saturdays when HELP arranges visits. We never just pop in unexpected. And Mrs. Finkell's not talkative anyway."

"Could you mention my concern to your pastor?" He fell back against the cushion, sipped the tea, and waited.

"Sure," she said, studying his worried face. "You must think it's serious."

"I don't know." A thoughtful frown appeared. "Something didn't look right to me."

"You're as bad as I am. You can't leave your work at the office."

"I think you're worse," Scott said. "I've never known anyone like you to want to do things for others. Constantly. You spend all day with those poor kids and then volunteer—"

"They're not poor kids, Scott. They're fighters. They're victims of circumstances. Most of the kids are bright and loveable—"

"I'm sorry, Kate. I chose the wrong word. I'm sure they're great kids…but you're so devoted, you don't have a life for yourself."

Scott's voice faded as a startling insight struck him. Was this the reason she'd never married? She was so busy with other people's children that she didn't have time for her own.

"The children need someone to give them hope. Someone who soothes their hurts and shows compassion and love. That's why I'm devoted."

Scott sensed he should shut his mouth. In some unknown way, he'd overstepped his boundaries or hit upon something that bothered her. Part of the paradox intrigued him. "Let's talk about something else," he suggested. "Why don't you come over here?" He patted the sofa beside him. "You look tense."

She didn't move. "I feel bad for those kids, Scott."

"I know you do. Neither of us like it. We just react differently. I'm a doctor, but I try not to let those situations get me down. You should, too."

"I need to pray that I learn to do that," she said.

"You can," Scott said. "It takes practice." He gave her a cockeyed smile.

A faint smile rose on her lips, and Scott whispered up a word of thanks. The last thing he wanted to do was upset her—and without knowing why.

He slapped the cushion again. "Get over here."

"Why?" she asked. Her chin jutted forward with a "make me" expression.

Scott drew in a relieved breath, sensing he'd distracted her from whatever bothered her. Teasing, he pushed his hands against the cushion, lifting himself an inch above the sofa. "Do I have to come there and get you?"

A full grin shuffled to her face, and she rose from the chair and inched across the carpet, closing the distance between them. "I'm here. So what do you want? More tea?"

He clasped her arm and pulled her to his side, shifting her sideways so he faced her back, then lifted his hands to the tightened cords in her neck and shoulders. "You need to relax."

As his fingers kneaded her taut muscles, his own body reacted at his action. What was he doing? His pulse skipped, then raced up his arm and his chest fluttered inside like a kite, dipping and soaring, on the wind.

As his fingers worked their miracle, a soft, contented moan escaped Kate's throat. She leaned into him, her head rocking from side to side in rhythm to the music that wrapped around them.

"Feel good?" Scott whispered.

"Mmm-hmm," she murmured, seeming to enjoy the melodic silence that blanketed them.

Kate shifted toward him as if his question had broken the intimate spell that bound them. "Thanks. That was wonderful."

Her gaze caught him unaware, and longing rose to his chest. Her mouth was pink and inviting, and as his yearning grew, he relished the thought of its tender sweetness.

Her lips parted appearing to speak, but she only studied him as if reading his thoughts.

Self-control and good sense rode off on the rhythmic waves of comfortable stillness. Scott lowered his mouth to hers, tenderly, his heart thundering like the ocean tide crashing to shore.

A silent gasp moved against her lips, maddening his senses. When he withdrew, her eyes drifted open, glazed with anxious surprise.

Kate shifted backward, but her gaze remained locked to his. No words, only a soft melody filled the air. Then a delicate pink flush rose to her cheeks, and she evaded him.

When she moved to rise, Scott caught her hand. "I hadn't planned that, Kate. It just happened." He longed to see approval in her eyes.

She bit the corner of her lip, the color now heightened, he hoped, from their kiss, and he yearned to cover her mouth with his, again.

"You've addled me. I hadn't expected…I didn't think that…" She inched away from him, her hands clutched at her waist. "It makes living in the same house difficult."

Was she right? "I'm sorry, Kate. I didn't mean to complicate things."

"You surprised me, that's all."

He wanted to hear her say that his kiss touched her as it had him.

"I don't think it should happen again, Scott. It's…for the best."

His heart sank to his feet. This wasn't what he wanted to hear. Not at all.

* * *

"I'm sorry you're still having bad dreams, Amber," Kate said, leaving her desk and crouching beside the tearful child. "Are you sure you can't remember even one?"

She wagged her head from side to side, wiping tears from her eyes with the back of her hand.

Kate moved her fingers in gentle, soothing circles across the child's back. For the past month, Amber's nightmares had darkened the child's world. If Kate had any clue as to the content of Amber's dreams, she might be able to explain them away. But all Kate had learned in their time together was that Amber found comfort in the stuffed lamb that she'd handed her the first day they'd met.

"Are you okay now?" Kate asked.

Amber tilted her head upward. "Yes."

"I have a present for you."

"For me?" The child's eyes widened.

Kate rose from her stooped position, swallowing her emotion, and grasped the package from the top of the filing cabinet. "Here you go." She placed the box in the child's lap and propped herself against the desk.

Amber peered at the gift, then raised her questioning face to Kate's.

"You can open it," Kate said, love and concern dominating her senses.

A faint grin etched Amber's disbelieving countenance. With timidity, she tugged at the corner of the wrapping and freed the box. Lifting the lid, her face brightened. "Sparky!" She lifted out the floppy-eared stuffed animal. "My own puppy."

"*Sparky?* You thought of a name already?"

Amber cradled the toy against her chest. "Uh-huh."

"I had a dog when I was your age. A real one," Kate said.

"You did?"

"Sure did. A spaniel with droopy ears like this one."

Amber cradled the stuffed toy against her chest. "I love him." In the sunlight glinting through the window, Amber's hazel eyes sparkled with flecks of gold. "Thank you."

Kate walked around the desk and sat. She rested her back against the chair, her emotions too tangled with the child's. "Time's about up, Amber. But remember if you have any more bad dreams, they're not real. They go away when you wake up." She glanced toward the doorway and softened her voice. "And don't forget to ask Jesus to watch over you and chase away your scary dreams, okay?"

Amber nodded. "Okay," she echoed.

Kate rose from her chair and rested her hand on the child's shoulder. "You can take the puppy to your room if you'd like."

"Can I leave him here? Cuz he's safe with you."

Tears pushed at the back of Kate's eyes. "I'll take good care of him. Whenever you're ready, he'll be waiting for you."

"Okay," Amber said as she slid off the chair.

Angry at herself for letting her feelings surface, Kate walked the child to the doorway. "See you next week, and don't forget, if you need me, I'm here."

Amber nodded, then turned and marched down the hallway toward her classroom.

Watching her bouncing blond curls, Kate wiped the stray tears from her eyes. Her feelings were not good. Getting herself in an emotional tizzy over Amber was in no one's best interest.

But her aching heart didn't have a choice. As soon as the child had stepped into her office, a medley of sensations churned in her chest. Concern, curiosity, tenderness and love. Kate's empty arms, longing for her own child, yearned to mother the girl and protect her from hurt. And those dreams? What caused Amber's fearful nightmares? Kate longed to talk to the grandmother. She'd be the one to fill in the gaps of Amber's memory.

Kate's mind churned with speculation throughout the day, and when she arrived home filled with questions, she waited for Scott.

After dinner, Kate cornered him alone in the living room. "Can I get your opinion about something?"

"Sure."

"I've told you about Amber," she said, sinking into the chair.

"Right, and if you want my opinion, you're getting too close, Kate. You'll get hurt."

Kate's heart rose to her throat, and she swallowed. "That's not the opinion I needed." Again, his words closed the gate between them. If she didn't need his help, she wouldn't have asked.

His focus dropped to the carpet. "Sorry."

"She has dreams. Nightmares, really. Denise, that's her housemother, says she often wakes at night in tears, but Amber has no recollection of her nightmares."

Scott lifted his gaze and a scowl creased his forehead. "You've asked her?"

"Yes, she tells me she can't remember. I'm not sure if that's true or if she doesn't want to remember."

"How about trying association? Words that might trigger a repressed event."

Kate considered what he'd said. "I don't know. Maybe, but I'm sure the grandmother could tell me." She bit her lower lip in thought. "I don't suppose the Haven director would let me take Amber to the hospital for a visit."

"And I think he'd be right. She hasn't adjusted to the Haven, yet." He rubbed the back of his neck. "Better hang on for a while. Maybe the grandmother will rally, or once Amber's more adjusted, she might be allowed a visit."

The real question she wanted to ask niggled at her. She already sensed what his reaction would be, but she had to ask. Scott was her only hope. "Until I can visit the grandmother, maybe you could do me a favor."

His suspicious eyes captured hers.

She hesitated. "Well…you work at County General, and, uh, could you, maybe, read her file? Something in it might—"

"I can't do that, Kate." He nailed her with his gaze. "I have access to my patient charts, but I can't scout around the hospital reading files."

"But if you heard something…or maybe asked around."

He shook his head, his lips compressed and drawn. "I'm too new there, Kate. Maybe after I've been there awhile, but for now, sorry, I just can't."

"Sorry about what?" Phyllis asked from the doorway. She faltered, then inched into the room. "Looks like I arrived in time for an argument."

"Not an argument," Scott said.

"No? I never have any fun." Phyllis sank into the cushion beside him.

Scott reached over and rumpled her hair, then told her Kate's request. Though she sided with Kate, it was obvious Phyllis could see her brother's side, also.

Kate leaned against the chair, studying the honest exchange between brother and sister, so alike, yet so different. She'd never noticed before how unalike they were in appearance. Though Phyllis was tall, she was trim and small boned. Scott, on the other hand, was muscular and solid. And their coloring and features…

"What's so interesting? You're staring."

Discomfort skittered up Kate's back. She disliked

people who gawked, and now she was doing the same. "I was noticing how different you are. Not opinions…" She gave them an arched brow. "But looks. No one would know you're related."

"We're not," Scott said.

His abrupt comment startled Kate. She eyed him, expecting to see a smile, but he wasn't smiling. "You're disowning her because she took my side?"

"No," he said, matter-of-factly. He glanced at Phyllis, a quizzical expression on her face. "Apparently, she doesn't know."

Phyllis shrugged. "Never came up in conversation."

Kate's heart thudded against her breastbone, wondering where the conversation was leading. She looked for a joke in their cryptic comments. But they weren't smiling. "You're not making sense."

"I'm adopted, Kate," Scott said.

Chapter Four

An unsettled feeling slid through Scott as he assayed Kate's surprised face. Her look seemed more than surprised. Maybe startled, apprehensive, frightened. But why? He watched her struggle to regain composure, and his mind whirled in its own confusion, wondering what to say.

"We shocked you, I guess," he said finally.

Her paled complexion revitalized, and her wide-eyed stare wilted. "No, I'm, uh, just…really surprised. Certainly not shocked. I don't, well, I'm confused why, uh, this never came up in any conversation."

Phyllis responded, her face as mystified as Scott felt. "It's not something Scott and I think about, Kate. We've been brother and sister since I was born." She turned to Scott as if pleading for support.

"I suppose it's difficult to understand unless

you've been there. I wasn't even four when Phyllis was born.''

Phyllis chuckled. ''You think you're surprised. Imagine how Mom and Dad felt when they thought they'd never have a birth child...and I came along.''

Scott joined her good humor. ''She's my sister...only different parents.''

As if tempering her comment, Kate lifted her hand to her lips. ''I'm sorry to act so stupefied. You really threw me, that's all.''

Unsure how to handle the situation, Scott gave her a grin that he hoped was playful and drew a cross with his index finger above his heart. ''Promise. We have no more skeletons in our closet.''

Beyond the flicker of a grin, Kate didn't respond.

''And speaking of closets,'' Scott said, grappling to change the subject, ''who wants to go over the apartment ads with me? There has to be a place somewhere in this area that can pass our inspection.''

''I vote for Kate,'' Phyllis said, rising. ''I have some laundry to do.''

Laundry? Knowing it was a feeble excuse, Scott watched his sister leave the room. ''You're stuck,'' he said to Kate whose natural coloring had returned.

''I could do some laundry, too, you know,'' she said, her tone once again droll.

''Let's put it this way,'' he countered. ''The longer I wait to find an apartment, the longer I'll live here with you.''

''Well, if you put it that way,'' she said, rising

and settling beside him on the sofa, "where's that paper?"

She shot him a bright smile, and he sent one back. But his comment hit him like a wrecker's ball. When he found an apartment, would Kate ease out of his life? Would the distance send her deeper into her secret world—a world that confused him, yet a world he wanted to understand?

Trudging up the final flight of stairs, Kate studied Scott as he reached the landing ahead of her. They had looked at two unacceptable apartments, and she hoped this time her prayers would be answered—a decent rental. She needed to get away from him before her emotions were too tightly wrapped around his.

Besides, she was irritated. She'd asked one favor of him—to help her check the records of Amber's grandmother. He'd refused. Now, here she was like a fool on a sunny Saturday afternoon, dragging her body up another narrow stairway to view an apartment.

"I'm wearing you out," Scott said as she reached the landing. "This is 3A right here. Front of the building for a change."

He took the key he'd picked up from the super and turned it in the lock. When he pushed open the door, Kate scanned the room. For once, bright sunshine poured in from two large windows. But the light emphasized the less than clean walls and carpet. She debated if Scott had noticed. His grimace answered her question.

"You could ask them to paint," she said, before Scott could mutter his contempt for the dirt. "At least the room has nice wide windows." *Dirty* windows, she added in her distressed ruminations.

Kate stepped into the kitchen where the grime seemed more pronounced. Grease glazed the wall behind the range and the stove top was dulled with dirt. "A little elbow grease will help," she said, turning to face an empty room.

Scott had already moved on ahead of her. She followed the sound of his footsteps down the short hall: bath on one side and bedroom on the other.

Defeat. She saw it in his face. "Let's have lunch and regroup," Kate said.

Without question, he headed back toward the living room and into the building hallway. She bounded behind him down the stairway, wishing he'd at least say something. His silence left her feeling disheartened.

After returning the key, they headed outside and sank into the car seats.

"We're going about this wrong," Kate said.

Finally Scott spoke. "Sorry I'm so down. You can tell me what I'm doing wrong while we grab a bite."

She had said what *we're* doing wrong, but she bit back the correction.

Without waiting for her response, he pulled away and drove in silence.

Nearing the downtown Royal Oak eateries, Scott seemed to pull himself from his doldrums. "I need fresh air. I thought we'd go to one of the cafés in town."

They were nearly there, and Kate felt no need to reply.

He parked the car on Center Street, and they headed for Main Street. The sidewalks bustled with pedestrians ogling the boutique windows and sitting beneath wide, colorful umbrellas.

Scott flagged a hostess, and they were seated at a cozy outdoor table.

The green covering only blocked half the warm July sun, and the rays felt pleasant, warming her arms from the car's air-conditioning. Scott reached into his shirt pocket and pulled out sunglasses, sliding them on his nose while he perused the menu. After a moment, he laid it on the table.

"I hope this place is okay, Kate," he said, looking at her for the first time since they'd left the apartment building. "I didn't ask, did I?"

"No, but this place is okay. Don't worry. We all have bad days," Kate said, not wanting him to feel worse. His bright smile and good nature was Kate's personal dose of medicine. Seeing him depressed stirred her own deeper sadness.

A pleasant breeze ruffled the umbrellas, and the rich aroma of food hung on the summer air. Her stomach stirred and she focused on the menu, instead of Scott's unusually serious face.

When the waiter arrived, Kate ordered a chef

salad and Scott, a stacked sandwich. Their sodas were delivered within a minute, and Kate took a sip before she began.

"What are you thinking?" she asked, organizing the musings she had earlier.

Behind his sunglasses, his eyes were hidden, but he lifted his face from the tumbler to hers. "That's the problem. I'm not sure what's bothering me. The sad state of those apartments or…what?"

"What you need first is to find a roommate, I think. Someone to share expenses. Then you can handle a higher rent and find a better place."

"Probably," he mumbled, preoccupied with stirring the drink with a straw. "I like your house. You have room and a yard. I suppose I'm depressed with the idea of being cramped up in a small space again. The rental prices around here are out of sight."

"Then why look for a place now? You've only been here a few weeks. Wait until you meet someone who'd like to share expenses."

To Kate's relief, he pulled off his sunglasses and leaned forward, searching her eyes. "Are you saying I can stay at the house until then?"

His question settled in her empty stomach like a block of ice. The answer *yes* fluttered to her tongue, but wisdom froze the words in her throat.

"I love staying with you and Phyllis, but you'd prefer me gone, I think." He inched even closer. "Be honest, Kate."

The ice melted with his warmth, and unexpected pleasure bubbled in her thoughts, running over into her words. "Sure, you can stay. I can't throw you out on your ear, can I?" Her pulse surged through her like a burst of steam.

Her hand rested on the table, and he slid his palm toward her and covered her fingers. "Are you positive?"

Unbidden happiness eased down her limbs. "Have I ever been anything but positive?"

Her double meaning brought a smile to his drawn lips. A blast of air shot from his chest and a rich laugh followed. "I feel better already."

At his words, the waiter arrived with their order. While he set their plates on the table, Kate grasped at the seconds to control her wavering emotions. She had just done the opposite of what she had prayed. Why?

Voices of other patrons filled her ears, and she reflected on the nearby window boxes filled with contained flowers reaching toward the light. Was she like those restricted blossoms bound in their small compartments, stretching and yearning for the sun?

She had suppressed her life, focusing on her work and her home. Not much else, except Phyllis who'd been a good friend. But life offered so much more if she weren't so fearful of facing the dark recesses of her past. She sensed God had forgiven her, but she hadn't forgiven herself. How long would she punish herself for her youthful mistake?

"Not hungry?" Scott asked.

She jerked inwardly hearing his voice and realized she'd drifted off in contemplation. "I was admiring the flowers," she said, stretching the truth.

She lifted her fork and dug into the appetizing salad. The large plate brimmed with fresh lettuce and sliced egg with julienne-cut meats and cheeses. The creamy dressing and savory meat dropped to her tongue and reminded her how hungry she really was.

She lifted a crusty roll from the small plate and broke a piece, using it to scoop her salad onto the fork. Her gaze lifted to Scott, opening his mouth to a mile-high sandwich. She laughed at his antics and felt her shoulders ease and soften to relaxed comfort.

When he'd consumed half the deli sandwich, Scott leaned back and plucked a large curly potato chip from his plate. "Did you talk to the pastor yet?" he asked, then bit into the chip.

Kate swallowed and wiped her mouth with the paper napkin. "Pastor Ray, you mean?"

"Right. About visiting the woman I mentioned."

Kate chuckled. "Mrs. Finkell. No, HELP hasn't met again. Next Saturday's our usual weekend. Are you coming along?"

"If I'm not working." His face grew serious. "I'm really concerned about her, Kate. For some reason, I keep thinking about the lady."

"I haven't mentioned anything to Pastor Ray, but I can if you're that worried."

"Would you? I'd be relieved."

Kate watched him tackle the sandwich again and thought about his concern. She had to admire Scott's dedication. The elderly woman had absorbed him since the day he'd met her. Kate reflected on the Haven and her own worries about the children and families with whom she worked. Perhaps she was as devoted as Scott and didn't recognize it.

As Kate forked into her salad, faces of the helpless children whom she'd talked to over the past months marched through her thoughts until Amber rose and settled in her mind. The child's fears and nightmares concerned Kate. She had to do something to find out more about the girl. And if Scott wouldn't help her, then she'd take it into her own hands. The significant thing was to help Amber.

Feeling resentful, Scott stood in the hospital cafeteria line. He'd gotten stuck working the weekend. And today, Kate was off with the HELP group—to his surprise, where he wanted to be. Worry for Mrs. Finkell rattled through him, but was quickly replaced by Kate's glowing image.

He drifted back to when he'd spent his first full day in her company. A day that changed his life. He'd always concentrated on his career—except for the unpleasant involvement with Lana in college. But since Kate literally charged into his life, he'd found his focus wavering. Wise or not.

Since then, Kate's image pervaded all hours of his day and night. He'd lain in bed knowing she was one floor below him. Some mornings at breakfast, he'd seen her wrapped in a long-sleeved, belted robe with a delicate sheer, pink hem peeking beneath.

The picture stirred him as he tried to sleep, thinking she was as soft and fragile as the cloth. And he longed that her inner reflections were as revealing as he imagined her gown.

At the cashier, he eyed his tray, amazed that he'd selected items from the counter while he'd been pre-occupied with Kate. He glanced at the filled tables and spotted one unoccupied chair at a table for two.

"Do you mind?" he asked the doctor seated in the other chair.

"Not at all," the man said, jutting his hand forward. "Cass Wentworth."

"Scott Ryan," he said, taking the doctor's hand in a firm shake. He set down his tray and slid into the chair.

"You're new to County General," the young doctor stated.

"Yes, I'm a resident. What service are you in?"

"Internal medicine. I'm up on medical."

"Do you care for stroke patients, by chance?" Scott asked, Kate entering his mind again.

"No, County General has a Stroke Unit. Why? Do you know someone there?"

Scott shook his head. Kate's request weighed on his shoulders. Why hadn't he told her he'd see what he could do? "A friend has interest in a patient there."

"Ah," he said, without further questions.

The young doctor was amiable, and as they chatted, Scott enjoyed his good humor and was grateful to learn a little of the hospital scuttlebutt.

"Where do you live?" Cass asked, tilting his tumbler to drain the last of his juice.

A feeling of discomfort settled over Scott. "Well, I'm, uh, looking. I'm staying with a relative." Annoyed at his own foolish evasiveness, Scott added, "My sister. She and a friend have a house."

"That's worked out for you?"

"I can't stay there. I need to find a place...one of these days."

Cass sat for a moment without comment, then, as if he had settled his thoughts, he focused on Scott. "I'm considering taking in someone to share my condo. I thought I'd enjoy the privacy, but I feel like I'm rattling around in it."

"Where is your place?" Scott asked, wondering if Cass was suggesting the possibility of rooming with him.

"Downtown Royal Oak. Great location. Close to the freeway. You'll have to stop by sometime. See what you think." He rose, lifted his tray with his left hand, and extended his other to Scott. "Nice to meet you."

"Thanks," Scott said, reciprocating. "Maybe, I'll do that."

Cass backed away. "Medical's on the fifth floor. Drop by. I'll show you around." He gave Scott a nod and headed for the tray conveyer and the door.

His proposition settled on Scott like a stamping press. Now that Kate had offered the surprise suggestion that he stay at the house for a while, he'd been in no hurry. Still, Kate's offer had landed in his lap as gently as dandelion parachutes. And possibly as fragile. A wind of misunderstanding could blow the proposal away.

He tucked away Cass's proposition. He didn't know the man well enough to grasp if the offer was serious or just an offhanded comment. He'd think about it later.

"Anyway, we had a great day," Kate said, noticing Scott's silence while she related their HELP chores. She recalled her curiosity that morning. When Kate arrived at Mrs. Finkell's, she'd studied the woman, looking for a clue to Scott's concern. Nothing caught her attention. She didn't understand Scott's insistence to ask the pastor about his disquiet.

"Oh," she added, "and Pastor Ray said he'll find some way to thank us for all our hard work over the summer."

"Did he say anything else?" Scott asked. His pinning gaze confirmed what he meant.

"Well," Kate complied, "if you mean about visiting Mrs. Finkell, he didn't say no, but he did say that you should telephone first. And to make sure you have a legitimate reason to visit other than checking on her health."

Scott's shoulders lifted and his voice sizzled with irritation. "Why else would I go to visit her, Kate? Did you tell him I'm a doctor?"

Phyllis jumped in. "He knows that Scott, but you aren't Mrs. Finkell's doctor."

"You can't just knock on someone's door and do a physical examination," Kate added.

"Thank you, ladies, for your wisdom." He shook his head and sank back against the chair. "I have better sense than that. I'll think of something."

A lengthy silence filled the room, and Kate squirmed against the upholstery, brooding over Scott's aloof manner. A month ago, his distraction would be the answer to her prayer, but now, events had changed that. Instead, longings shifted through her. Hopeless, useless fantasies. And no matter how hard she tried to convince herself, the dream remained. She liked Scott more than she wanted to admit.

"Who's hungry?" Phyllis asked, breaking the silence. She rose and took a step toward the kitchen.

Kate only cleared her throat, longing to stay quiet until she heard what Scott would say. But he remained silent and thoughtful.

Finally Kate gave in. "I suppose we should eat something."

Scott rose and stretched his arms above his head. "I think I'll skip dinner. The hospital staff's softball team plays tonight."

"Okay," Phyllis said, disappearing through the doorway.

"Softball. Sounds like fun," Kate said. Holding her breath, she waited like a child listening to the distant chimes of an ice cream truck.

"I'll pick up a sandwich or something," he said, feeling the back pocket of his jeans as if checking for his wallet. He patted the spot, then stepped to the door.

Filled with disappointment, Kate watched, willing him to turn around and invite her. When he paused and faced her, she froze in place.

"You're welcome to come along…if you'd like." He looked at her with question.

Suspended, she caught her breath, then rose. "A sandwich and softball? What could be better?" She smiled.

"Better? Not much, except add a soda…and your smile." His apprehensive expression changed to a grin.

"And you," he added, sliding his arm around her shoulder.

At that moment, Kate forgot about the sandwich, soda and softball. The only part that hung in her thoughts was, "And you."

Chapter Five

Clutching their fast-food bag in his left hand, Scott steered Kate along the Boulan Park bleachers until they found space on a lower bench. As he opened the sack, he glanced at the scoreboard.

"County General's behind," he told Kate.

"Losing? Who are they playing?"

"Beaumont Hospital. They're our major competitor." Scott handed her a wrapped burger and a soda. He rolled down the top of the bag and slipped it between them. "I left the fries inside." He used his elbow to point.

Kate nodded, her eyes directed toward the team. "Who's up?" she asked.

"Beaumont, but..." He watched the shortstop leap backward and snatch the ball. "Out!" he yelled. "Third out. We're up."

As the teams shifted places on the diamond, Scott

spied a familiar face among the team members. He jostled Kate's arm. "See the tall guy warming up over there—with the bats?"

Kate nodded.

"I met him in the cafeteria today. Cass... Wentworth, I think he said. Nice guy. Works on the medical floor." Scott didn't mention Cass's comment about sharing his place. Though he hadn't expected it, the idea left an empty feeling in his chest.

Though Cass's words lingered, the lively game soon captured Scott's attention again. He munched on the fries and swallowed the burger amid his boisterous yells, and soon Kate joined in, getting caught up in the excitement. Her cheeks glowed in the orange rays of the sinking sun. When she cheered as County General moved ahead of Beaumont, she turned to him with sparkling eyes and a brilliant smile.

"We're winning," she yelled, swinging so quickly toward Scott she sloshed some soda on her leg.

Scott snatched a roll of carry-out napkins from his pocket and pressed them against her jeans. She stretched her slender limb forward as he dabbed while they laughed at her exuberance.

"You can dress her up, but you can't take her out," Scott said, dragging the old saying from the recesses of his memory—the way his father always teased his mother.

Kate responded with a grin, but with the rousing

yells, she leaped from the bench as a home run added a point to the winning score.

When the cheering died down, Scott rose and gathered the trash while Kate stood and eyed her damp jeans. While they maneuvered through the crowd, Scott tossed the garbage in a basket, then turned and found himself facing his new friend.

"Scott," Cass said.

"Hey, great game." Scott gave Cass's shoulder a friendly shake, then noticed Cass eyeing Kate.

"Cass, this is my friend Kate Davis. She's my, uh, room…" Flustered, he hesitated. "I think I mentioned that I live with my sister and Kate."

"Ahh," he said, flashing Scott a wry smile.

"No," Scott said. "We're just friends."

"No wonder you didn't jump at my offer," Cass continued, as if not listening.

Kate's voice lifted in question. "Offer?"

"I didn't realize it *was* an offer," Scott countered, uncomfortable with the direction of the conversation. Feeling the need to explain, he turned to Kate. "Cass mentioned he's considering sharing his condo."

Her curiosity seemed to shift to rigid politeness. "That's nice."

Seeming unaware of the tension, Cass looked from one to the other. "Are you headed anywhere? My place is only a few miles from here—Crooks Road to Main Street. How about following me home, and you can see the place?"

Scott's stomach tightened. Instead of feeling the

pleasure of finding his own place, disappointment reared inside him. He peered at Kate. "What do you say?"

Her expression was unreadable.

"Sure," she said. "That'd be nice." As if miles away, she stared at the ground.

Was she disappointed? The question bounced through Scott's head. If so, then perhaps she cared more than she let on. Why did he care anyway? He chided himself for his stupid question. He knew why. He liked Kate. More than liked her, Scott was fond of her. He drew in a ragged breath. *Fond?* Why was he playing games with himself?

When he focused, Cass stared at him curiously.

"Well?" Cass asked.

"Sure. Why not?" Scott said. Placing his hand against Kate's back, he guided her to follow Cass toward the parking lot.

The ride from Boulan Park passed quickly, and when they entered the parking lot, Scott scanned the attractive condos that were designed like a neat row of New England two-story bungalows.

"Not bad," Scott said, pulling into a space near Cass.

Kate was quiet.

He opened his door, but Kate exited the passenger side before he could be a gentleman. When Cass joined them, Kate finally spoke.

"I hope I'm not in the way," she said to Cass.

"Heavens, no. I like having pretty ladies around."

The comment may have been innocent, but Scott tensed at Cass's obvious flirtation. Yet, he'd given the man an open invitation by referring to Kate as a friend.

As Kate walked beside Cass to the front door, Scott straggled behind. The two chatted amiably, Scott's presence unnoted. He felt like the outsider and didn't like the feeling. An uneasy sensation prickled his awareness. Cass's comment that he liked pretty women hanging around didn't set well. Did he mean overnight?

And Kate. He studied her, curious if she was returning Cass's interest. Old memories tugged at him. He'd trusted Lana and she'd betrayed that trust.

Cass held the door, waving him in, and Scott followed Kate into a sunny living room. Scott admired the masculine, comfortable area in shades of beige and browns with a bit of rusty red like an old brick. Leather furnishings formed a U-shape and faced a large cabinet where, Scott guessed, he would find a television and CD equipment behind closed doors.

"Nice," Scott said, knowing his co-worker expected him to say something.

"Thanks. I like it," Cass said, turning toward a doorway.

Kate oohed her pleasure over the kitchen with plentiful oak cabinets and almond accessories. A bay window nook held an oak table and chairs.

The second floor housed two large bedrooms with private baths and an open sitting area between. Against one wall, a large oak stand held Cass's computer and printer. A perfect setup, yet Scott found himself searching for problems. He found none.

When they returned to the first floor and accepted Cass's invitation for a soda, they settled in the living room.

"What do you think?" Cass asked. "Roomy enough, I think. Did you see the guest bath off the laundry room?"

Kate chuckled. "This is almost as large as my whole house."

With both pairs of eyes on him and nothing negative to use as an excuse, Scott admitted it was a great place. Still, a nagging feeling caused him to hesitate. What about Cass's overnight guests?

"Would you like to give it a try, Scott?" Cass asked.

"Hmm? It's hard to refuse," he said, still struggling with his thoughts.

"Hard to refuse, but I hear some hesitation," Cass said. "I suppose I don't blame you when you can wake up in the morning to a pretty face like this one." Sitting with Kate on the sofa, Cass nestled his hand against her shoulder. "You're much more attractive than I am."

A pink flush rose up her neck while heat boiled up Scott's spine.

Bristling with indignation, Scott revealed his agitation. "I'm wondering if you have the wrong idea, here."

A puzzled expression covered Cass's face. "What idea?"

"I'm not involved with Kate...if that's what you think." Defending his morals, he'd done it again— let Cass think that Kate meant nothing to him.

Cass fell back against the cushion and lifted his hands in defense. "Whoa, man, I'm sorry if I suggested that. I'm just toying with Kate. I really didn't mean to offend either of you."

Kate's befuddled countenance oscillated like a tennis match spectator's, as she pivoted her head from one to the other.

"You didn't offend me, but..." Scott didn't know what to say. Humiliation slithered up his spine, and he faced a shocking insight. In his heart, Kate was his. No action, words or obvious truth to his feeling, but that's exactly how he felt. "I'm not comfortable with 'toying' around, I guess."

His concerned expression fading, Cass's face filled with good humor. "I get it. Are you worried about me having babes hanging around...night and morning?" He peered at Scott. "I admit I'm a tease, but it stops there. I know that's odd for this day and age, but..."

Cass hesitated, glancing at Kate. "I'm embarrassed to admit this, but I, uh, sort of believe that a real commitment...I suppose I should say marriage, is the time for being intimate."

Scott clamped his mouth from gaping at Cass's words. "You're kidding?"

Discomfort crept to Cass's face. "No, I'm serious."

"Who'd have thought? I agree. That conviction

has gotten me into trouble, but to me, chastity's a precious gift between husband and wife."

"My thoughts exactly. So, now that we have that settled, are you interested?" Cass chuckled. "The day we met in the cafeteria, you struck me as an easygoing guy—one I'd enjoy sharing the place with."

"You mean I made an impression on you that fast?"

Cass grinned.

With mixed feelings, Scott struggled to respond. "Well, sure…I'd, uh, like to give it a try. We need to talk rent, but…other than that, why not?"

Scott knew why not, but it wasn't a logical reason. He had no assurance that Kate gave a hoot about him. Why open himself up for hurt again? He didn't need it.

Wondering why she'd been so quiet, Scott looked at Kate. A strange sadness loomed on her face, seeming pale in the lamplight. When he caught her attention, she looked as if she'd been pronounced guilty of some heinous crime.

A weight settled on his shoulders. What had he said or done to cause her to look utterly defeated?

Kate rolled over on her bed and wiped her eyes with the corner of her wilted T-shirt. Friday night and the house was empty, except for her. Earlier, Kate witnessed Phyllis's glowing face as she parading through the doorway on Darren's arm for a long-awaited date.

I'm happy for her, Kate thought, then cringed, hearing her own blatant lie. She knew in her heart she envied Phyllis like she had always envied her sister. Envy. If God wasn't merciful, she'd be in serious trouble.

And Scott. A rustle of tenderness drifted up her arms to her chest. Kate pictured his strong arms, muscles bulging as he toted luggage and boxes from the second floor to his car. Last Sunday, he had emptied the guest room and said goodbye. She hadn't heard a word.

Again, tears bubbled up and spilled down her cheeks. Self-pity. She hated it. Envy. She hated that, too. And that's what filled her—envy and self-pity. And where was her common sense? It had taken a vacation.

Scott's departure should have been a gift. But one that seemed a paradox, like a friend donating a kidney for you—a generous sacrifice, but a tremendous loss at the same time.

In her heart, she knew nothing could come of her relationship with Scott. She'd said it over and over. After their visit to Cass's place, Scott's words settled in her mind like the black plague. "Chastity is a precious gift between husband and wife."

The words struck Kate like an express train, and a deep sob erupted from her throat. She had no precious gift to offer anyone. With youthful ignorance and misplaced passion, she had given it away to a sturdy, good-looking football player. As if her treasure had been a meaningless gag gift, Ron threw it back in her face and walked away, leaving her with the tragic burden and sorrow.

Weighted by her melancholy, she folded her hands behind her head, struggling to control the rush of black memories that rolled through her like smoke from a house fire. The burning image seared her emotions and unable to bear the raging pain, she descended into uneasy sleep.

The telephone's ring pulled Kate from her bed like a police siren. She bolted upward, swung her legs from the mattress to the floor, and rose, grasping the nightstand to steady her reeling body. Her dark mood had settled on her like black fog, and in the unlighted bedroom, she stumbled her way to the door, then to the telephone.

"Hello," she said, her voice unsteady.

"Kate? Is something wrong?"

Her heart skipped as Scott's voice reconciled into reality. "No, I guess I fell asleep."

"See what happens when I move out. Life gets boring."

He chuckled, but his words hit Kate with dire truth.

Without waiting for her to respond, he continued, "Is HELP this weekend?"

"HELP? Ah, yes. Tomorrow." Her pulse raced at his question.

"Great. I have the day off. I'll come by and pick you up, okay?"

"Sure," she said, without thinking—without thinking wisely was more accurate.

"So, do you miss me?"

She faltered, wanting her heart to speak and not her brain. "It's quiet." *Quiet and empty.* The deep cavern of silence surrounded her.

"Sorry, I haven't called. It takes time getting to know a new housemate."

"I imagine." She regretted the bitterness that skipped through her voice.

"Are you okay, Kate?"

"I'm fine, really." Lie. Lie.

"If you're sure." He hesitated, then continued. "Cass is either dragging me out to dinner or filling me in on his life. Time flies. I really meant to telephone."

"I didn't expect you to call." Disgusting self-pity. She loathed it.

"But I meant to," he said, ignoring her response.

Kate grabbed herself mentally by the collar and gave herself a shake. "I'm glad you called, Scott. It does seem lonely here."

"If it weren't so late, I'd come by tonight, but tomorrow's not far away. I'll come by early."

"Okay," she said, longing to keep him on the telephone forever.

When he disconnected, Kate held the receiver, wanting to cling to the moment a little longer. No matter what she said or what her mind told her, she couldn't lose Scott's friendship. If nothing permanent could ever come of their relationship, she didn't care at the moment. He could be her friend. Her very dear friend. That's what she needed.

Chapter Six

Scott finished mowing Mrs. Finkell's lawn while the others completed the edging and trimming. Putting the mower back into Darren's truck bed, Scott wondered how the others would feel if he stayed behind to talk with the elderly woman. Her health concerns nagged at him. Being a doctor, he couldn't walk away without gathering some information.

When Kate came down the walk toward him, Scott's heart skipped a beat. Wondering what had happened, he studied her face. No matter what he said, she seemed tense and distant—nothing like the Kate he met a couple months earlier, flailing her flowered umbrella in his face. That day brightened in his memory, but seeing her now didn't. What could he do to bring back the Kate he once knew?

"Where's your smile, Katie?" he asked, sending her a toying smile.

Her gaze darted upward. "What?" A flickering grin settled on her lips. "How did you come up with that name?"

"I'm gifted, I suppose." He rested his hand on her shoulder. "I've missed you. Do you think it's true that absence makes the heart grow fonder?"

She gave him a swat and tossed her equipment in the truck. "Don't be silly."

But he watched the pleasure rise to her face. She missed seeing him every day, just as he missed her. He was certain.

Recalling his plan, he sidled over to her and lowered his voice. "Do you think Phyllis and Darren will mind if we lag behind so I can talk for a minute with Mrs. Finkell?"

"So that's why you're sweet-talking me," Kate said.

"No. That was the truth. This is a perfect opportunity to see the lady for a minute. You know I've been curious. What do you think?"

She shrugged. "I'm sure they'll understand."

To his relief, when Phyllis and Darren returned with their gear, they were in agreement.

"We won't be long," Scott promised. "Since she knows Kate, I figured she should be there."

Darren nodded as he stowed the gear in the truck bed. "See you in a while," he said, climbing into the cab. With a wave, they pulled away toward the next house.

When they were down the block, Kate headed up the sidewalk to the porch and rang the bell.

Mrs. Finkell answered the door, and when Kate said they had time for a short visit, the woman swung the door wide. "Come in," she said. Her watery eyes narrowed in the late summer sun and she hurried to close the door.

When he stepped inside, Scott scanned the small living room overburdened with lace doilies and dusty knickknacks. A knitted quilt lay over the arm of the sofa, and a bed pillow propped nearby led him to believe the woman napped there.

"Just move that stuff and find a seat," she said, waving her hand as if the magazines and clothing would vanish from the furniture.

Scott shifted a pile of newspapers, leaving a spot large enough for him and Kate to sit.

"Like a lemonade?" Mrs. Finkell asked. "Can't seem to get enough to drink myself."

Studying her with a doctor's eye, Scott tallied up another symptom: hazy eyes, thirsty and open sores that he noticed since they'd entered the house.

"Just half a glass would be nice," Kate answered.

Scott said he'd take the same, and Mrs. Finkell left the room.

Scott waited for the woman to be out of earshot, then leaned toward Kate. "Look at her legs when she comes back. She has open sores above her ankles and they aren't healing. I'd say she has diabetes," he whispered.

"How can you tell from that?" Kate asked with a voice much too loud.

Looking through the doorway, Scott noticed the

woman returning, and he signaled Kate. She slammed her mouth closed as Mrs. Finkell stepped into the room.

"Here you are," she said, handing each of them a partially filled tumbler. She stepped back and sank into a rocker that faced away from the window. "That bright sunlight's hard on these old eyes of mine. Can't look at it."

"And you said you're often thirsty," Scott said, initializing his concern.

"Seem to be," she said, then turned her attention to Kate. "Can't thank all you church people enough for all you've done around here. I'll be ninety-two my next birthday. What do you say to that?"

"I'd say you're young at heart, Mrs. Finkell," Kate said.

"Not so young anymore," the woman added. "Figure I don't have too much longer before I meet my Maker, but you know, it's a funny thing." She sent them an eager smile. "As much as I love the Lord, I love this life, too."

"Good for you," Scott said, pleased she'd left him an opening. His concern rose as she mentioned her symptoms. "If you want to be around a few more years, you need to take care of yourself."

"Oh, I know that. Sometimes I'm lonesome, but most times, I'm content, even if it's just enjoying my memories."

Scott wasn't put off by her diversion, not when he'd gotten this close. "When's the last time you saw your doctor, Mrs. Finkell?"

She tilted back in the wooden rocker and focused across the room.

Scott followed her line of direction and spotted a display of framed photographs. One looked like a young girl's senior picture.

The older woman gestured toward the bookcase. "That's my daughter's picture there. High school picture, but I always liked it." She looked down toward her gnarled fingers knotted in her lap. "Since she moved away, it's hard for me to get out. I don't get to the doctor often."

"I imagine you miss your daughter," Kate said, leaning forward from her seat.

"I do, yes. Life gets lonely without family. I have no one around here to run errands or get me where I need to go."

Scott opened his mouth, but Kate jumped in ahead of him.

"But anyone from HELP would be happy to give you a ride to the doctor or anywhere. All you have to do is ask."

A smile spread over her wrinkled face, and she propelled the chair in a gentle rocking motion. "That's mighty nice of you. Guess you've become like family."

Unable to contain himself, Scott announced he was a doctor. Feeling a poke to the ribs, he turned to Kate and winced at her glower. But he couldn't stop. His worry was too great. Touching on symptoms, she'd mentioned—her thirst and her eyesight—Scott pointed out the open sores on her legs.

"I'd recommend you make an appointment, Mrs. Finkell."

A new grin tugged at her creased face. "Then, I can tell that old geezer I have a good-looking young friend who's a doctor."

"You could," Scott said with a chuckle.

Kate was quiet, but Scott explained again his concern for her health while the older woman listened. After obtaining a promise that she'd call her physician, Scott rose and took her hand. "We'll call you Monday evening, okay, Mrs. Finkell?"

She agreed.

Kate jotted down the woman's telephone number, and with a hug, she said goodbye. Scott followed her to the door, washed in relief. His prayers of thanks rose, pleased that the elderly woman had listened.

Outside as they walked to the car, Kate squeezed his arm. "I should be angry at you, but I'm grateful. If you hadn't insisted, she might have ignored you."

Scott paused at the car door and tilted her chin upward. "Thanks. It's hard being a doctor and overlooking the obvious."

His words took a turn, and determination thrust him onward. "And there's another obvious, I can't overlook." His heart compressed. "You're upset with me, I think." He watched her struggle to pull her gaze from his.

"I'm upset with myself...not you," she said. Her face paled and her shoulders appeared tense.

Scott searched her face, longing to know what she

meant, but he sensed the distance rising between them. "I wish you could tell me," he said finally.

"It's not important. Really. Just some old trappings hanging on from my youth. Troubles I should have buried long ago. But nothing you can do."

"I don't want to lose your friendship, Kate. I like you too much to have you pull away from me, and I feel a wedge growing between us."

His distress spurred him forward like a foot pressing on an accelerator to race through a yellow light. "I'll be honest. I hated to move in with Cass, because I was afraid you'd drift away from me. I don't want that to happen."

"I'm not drifting. Look, we're standing here talking."

He felt her lie tangle around his heart. Unless God intervened, she was drifting away beyond his grasp like a helium balloon on the wind. An iron fence had risen between them. He could see her and hear her, but he couldn't draw her into his arms. And no matter how firmly he denied his desire, that's exactly where he wanted her to be.

God intervened. When his director called him into the office, Scott couldn't believe what he heard.

"Since you're going into family practice, I thought Children's Haven might be right up your alley."

Scott closed his gaping mouth. "For how long?"

"Well, Dr. Barlow will need a month or so to

recuperate after his surgery. So you'll be there at least five or six weeks, I'd guess.''

"Full-time?"

"No, not full-time. Monday, Wednesday and Friday. And then you'll be on call for emergencies. You can handle that I should think."

"Yes, no problem. The change will be interesting." The phrase amused him. Interesting. More like wonderful.

"Fine. You'll begin next Monday, then."

When he left the director's office, Scott smiled widely. If Kate planned to pull away from him, God had another idea. And Scott definitely gave God credit for the amazing event.

After he'd talked to Kate outside Mrs. Finkell's, Scott pulled out of his intellect every reason and incident he could conjure, trying to make some sense out of Kate's behavior. She'd always been a little unsure of herself. He blamed that on her shaky self-esteem. He hoped someday she'd realize what a charming, wonderful person she was.

But since the day Cass had invited them to see the condo, she'd grown more distant. He couldn't put his finger on it. He relived the day. She'd been quiet, he recalled, but once he invited her to the softball game, she seemed to perk up and really come alive at the game.

He chuckled remembering how she'd spilled her drink in her exuberance. His heart tripped again recalling how he'd blotted the soda from her shapely leg hidden beneath her jeans.

Was she upset because they'd gone to Cass's place? When he pictured her animation and smiles, hanging on Cass's every word, rivalry poked at him.

But the problem wasn't then. It happened later—later when she became silent and brooding. What had they talked about? His mind went blank.

At times, he'd thought she was angry because he had been unwilling to help her check Amber's grandmother's records. Then, had second thoughts.

That particular problem he would soon solve. Rumor had been circulating that he'd be going up to the medical floor on his next service. While on medical, dropping into the stroke unit would be easy. Maybe if he told Kate, she'd cheer up.

He grinned, imagining Kate's expression when he appeared unexpectedly at her office door the following Monday. The transfer to Children's Haven would be a secret from her until then.

When Scott peered through her office doorway, Kate's mouth opened like a hungry baby bird's—except no sound came from her lips.

Leaping from her desk, she shot toward him, her hand pressed against her chest, peering at him with disbelief.

"What are you doing here?" she asked.

She stood in front of him, inspecting his doctor's coat, then looked at him with question.

"I'm the Haven's new doctor," he said.

"New doctor? Where's Dr. Barlow?"

"Having surgery." He guided her back to her

desk, then dropped into a chair and explained. "I'll only be a here a few weeks, but I knew you'd be thrilled. Right, Katie?" He gave her a million-dollar smile and was relieved when she laughed.

"You're so silly," she said as her shoulders relaxed. "Let me break the news. You've arrived at a good time. This morning, I hear we have two suspected cases of chicken pox. I hope you've had them."

"I have, but thanks for the warning." He rose and rested his palms on her desk, facing her. "I just dropped by to say hi. But I suppose I'd better get back before I find a line of speckled youngsters waiting for the doctor."

At the door, he halted and turned around. "Lunch? Could we eat together...say about one?"

She hesitated before answering. "Sure. In the cafeteria."

When Scott disappeared, Kate fell against the chair and caught her breath. What would she do now? She had tried so hard to get him out of her mind. A useless task, but she'd made a valiant effort.

Now he was here where she'd be with him three days a week. How could she keep her feelings under control? Even today, seeing him in his doctor's coat sent warmth edging through her body.

Scott was always handsome, but in his doctor's coat, he exuded an air of confidence, yet kindness. The white color broadened his already wide shoulders, and his nutmeg hair and deep-brown eyes added the boyish charm she loved—not to overlook his teasing dimples and generous smile. She chided her gushing infatuation.

Still, she really admired him, longing to have Scott's control and poise. In her work, she displayed those attributes, knowing her job backward and forward. Even the unwanted surprises—unexpected problems or serious situations involving the children—those, she could handle.

But beyond her career, Kate lacked self-direction and control in her personal life. Her past rose up like a cobra, ready to strike her, poisoning her thoughts. Kate's memory dragged back to her teen years…and her sister.

Even in junior high, Kristin had been popular. Friends, boys and girls, dropped by or telephoned to make plans or to gossip. In high school, Kristin had a date for every dance or special occasion.

Shrinking with the memory, Kate missed her senior prom. Another horrible occasion arched its ugly head, recalling the time her mother had forced her to go to a junior high dance escorted by her cousin. Kristin made sure everyone knew. Kate had been mortified. Always, Kate longed to be her sister, willing to do anything to be like Kristin. And she did.

The same old shame rifled through Kate again. Why had she sinned? She had disobeyed God's will and her parents' trust. In her heart, Kate believed that Kristin had given herself to boyfriends. Kristin had been streetwise. Kate had been naive. All she had wanted was to be popular.

She closed her eyes and pushed the endless miseries into her Pandora's box. A deep sigh shuddered through her, and she looked at her wristwatch. Almost time for her next appointment. *Amber.* Her heart knotted as the child's image rose in her mind.

Kate stood and pulled Amber's stuffed dog from her bottom desk drawer. Placing it on her desk, she stretched her arms above her head. Sunlight spilled through the French pane window and etched her desktop with dark-edged boxes of sunshine. If she had to be in a box, let it be one filled with light.

As she stared at the pattern, a sound caused her to turn. Amber stood in her doorway, her face pale and drawn, her cheeks blotched with red.

"Don't you feel well?" Kate asked.

The child wandered in, rubbing her glazed eyes. "I'm not sick."

Kate heard her falsehood but didn't press the truth.

The girl headed for the familiar chair and slid to the seat. "I'm tired."

"I see. Why do you think you're tired?"

Amber shrugged, and Kate reached out and pulled the stuffed animal off her desk.

"Do you want to hold Sparky?"

The child nodded and took the stuffed animal in her lap. As she played with the floppy ears, Kate probed her for problems, asked about her dreams and allowed long pauses of silence to suspend on the air.

Realizing she was getting nowhere and worried about Amber's health, Kate rose and rested her hand on the child's shoulder. She inspected the girl's arms for spots, sensing that she might be coming down with chicken pox like the others had done. She saw nothing.

"Can I feel your forehead, Amber? You might have a fever," Kate asked.

She nodded, and Kate lay her palm across the child's brow and felt the heat she suspected.

"I think you have a little fever, sweetie," Kate said, stepping back and crouching in front of the girl.

Amber lifted her thoughtful eyes, her fingers still fiddling with Sparky's ears. "I remember something."

Kate's heart lurched. "About your dreams?"

A distant look washed over Amber's face. "No, not my dreams."

"No?" Kate said, holding her breath. "Then what?"

"I remembered I had a dog like Sparky once when I was a baby. He had long ears like this puppy."

"Are you sure?"

Her head nodded, convincingly. "I remember I cried."

"Did something happen to Sparky?" Kate's heart leaped, thinking if that event came to Amber's mind, maybe she would remember more.

"He ran away...." She paused, her eyes lifting to the ceiling, then back again. "Maybe, he died."

"Either one would make me sad, Amber." Kate

recalled how quickly Amber had named the stuffed toy. "Sparky" had flown out of the child's mouth. Could this be the beginning of her recollection?

Kate waited, but Amber didn't continue. "Is that all you remember?"

"I'm too tired." Amber leaned her flushed cheek against her shoulder.

Kate longed to take the child in her arms and hold her until every hurt was gone. But she knew better than to be too affectionate with the child. The Haven had rules. And it was best for Amber.

Kate rose and stepped backward. "Would you like to go to your room, Amber...or—" *Scott.* "Let's take a walk to the clinic. You can meet my friend. He's a doctor who'll be working here a few weeks. And he's very nice. What do you say?"

Amber lifted her glassy eyes and nodded.

Gesturing toward the door, Kate took a step forward, her heart riding on the waves of expectation. Amber could be in no better hands than Scott's. The image sifted through her and rolled into her consciousness. Kate's own problems assailed her like the plague. In whose hands would she be healed?

Chapter Seven

Scott rubbed the nape of his neck, then bent over the desk, filling in the medical chart of his third youngster that day diagnosed with chicken pox. If the housemothers didn't confine those children to an area, the Haven would have an epidemic on their hands.

Putting his clasped fingers behind his head, Scott leaned back in his chair and let his thoughts drift to earlier that morning. Kate's look of surprise amused him. But he wasn't positive that she had been pleased. Kate had a way of covering her true feelings, like a judge attempting to be fair and impartial.

When Scott tilted forward, he caught a glimpse of a small blond child beyond the doorway. When she entered the clinic, Scott was surprised to see Kate follow. Her expression was serious, and his attention returned to the child.

"Dr. Ryan, this is Amber," Kate said, maintaining a professional relationship.

"Hi, Amber," Scott said, observing the telltale flushed cheeks and glazed eyes. He could make this diagnosis in a heartbeat.

Kate continued, "I'm thinking she might—"

"Have chicken pox," Scott said. "If so, she's the fourth this morning."

"That's what I was afraid of," Kate said, biting her lip.

Amber was a pretty child. Her hair, lighter than Kate's, curled in a blond halo around her delicate features. She looked up at him with fearful, glassy eyes—vulnerable and fragile. Now, he understood why Kate seemed so drawn to the girl.

"Should I leave?" Kate asked.

"No, I need someone in the room." He grinned at her over his shoulder. "So you're it."

With Amber's focus riveted to her, Kate moved to a chair and sat.

Scott bent down and touched the child's mottled cheeks. "You're not feeling well, Amber?"

She took a faltering step backward and shook her head.

Scott straightened. "I need you up here," he said, patting the vinyl-covered table. "How about if I give you a boost."

Amber moved backward against Kate's knees, fear hovering in her eyes

"It's okay, sweetie," Kate said. "Remember. I told you the doctor's a friend of mine. He wants to see if you're getting chicken pox like some of the other kids."

Taking a cautious stride toward her, Scott extended his hand, and finally, she approached him and allowed Scott to lift her to the table.

He pulled the thermometer from a wall bracket and placed it in her mouth, then examined her neck and face. "Might be an early case? I don't see any polka dots." He winked at the girl.

Amber gave him a shy grin.

The thermometer gave a soft beep, and Scott removed it. "Hmm…102.8 Fahrenheit," he said aloud, for Kate's benefit. He leveled his eyes to Amber's. "No wonder you aren't feeling well, young lady."

"That's bad," Kate said.

He turned toward her. "For adults, but children's temps will often go higher." He pivoted back to Amber.

"Let's pull your T-shirt off, so I can check to see if you're turning into a spotted giraffe."

Giggling at his comment, Amber lifted her arms while Scott tugged off her pink shirt. Though a few faint rashes appeared on her skin, Scott's eyes were drawn to the withered skin below the left shoulder. An old burn scar.

He caught Kate's attention, flagging her to the table. She rose and joined him, staring at the puckered skin marring the soft pink flesh of the child's back.

Though startled at first, Kate's face furrowed with

concern, but Scott shook his head, discouraging her from making comment.

The tender look in her eyes tugged at his heart. Kate cared more than she should for the child...as she probably did for every child who came to her office. She was a gentle, warm woman and would make a good mother, he was sure.

Amber held her hands folded tightly in her lap, her slender back rigid.

Scott grasped her shirt from the tabletop. "Well, missy, I'd say you're about ready to turn into a spotted young lady."

"I am," Amber said. "Do I have chicken pox?"

"You sure do. I'm afraid you'll have to take it easy for a few days." He slipped the pink top over her head, and she tugged it down to her waist.

Scott hoisted her off the table and leaned his hip against the edge. "Amber, do you know how you got the scar on your back?"

Her soft brown eyes widened. She shook her head.

"Do you know what kind of scar it is?"

She pressed her lips together and shrugged before murmuring her response. "No."

But Scott wondered if she did. No sense forcing her at this point, but he was anxious to talk it over with Kate.

"You need to get to bed, little lady. I'll talk to..." He peered at Kate for the name of the housemother.

"Denise," Kate said.

Scott nodded. "I'll talk to Denise, Amber, and tell her how to take care of you. Okay?"

Amber remained silence.

With his thoughts whirring, Scott pressed Kate's shoulder. "It's nearly lunch. I'll take Amber back, and I'll meet you in the cafeteria."

With her attention focused on Amber, Kate only nodded.

"I have to talk to Amber's grandmother," Kate said. "Especially now that we saw the scar." Her chest ached from seeing the wound on Amber's delicate skin.

Scott took a swig of cola to help wash down the sandwich and responded. "Kate, don't be foolish and rush into anything. When I get back to the clinic, I'll review her files."

"I've already looked through her files. I didn't see anything about a scar. It's a burn scar, right?"

He nodded. "First degree."

"What would cause a burn like that?" Kate asked.

"I'm not sure. Children are known for pulling scalding hot pans over on themselves. If it was something thick, like chili maybe, that could cause a serious burn. Or playing with matches. Some of them start their bedclothes on fire."

"Then, the grandmother will know. I'm going to the hospital to see her." She stirred the noodles in her chicken soup, but instead of eating, she dropped the spoon. "Look, the Haven investigates situations all the time when the case calls for it. So I'll cut all the red tape and do it myself.''

"What happens if someone finds out?" Scott asked. "Can you get yourself in hot water?"

"No." She spit the word out, then thought better and shrugged. "Well...I shouldn't. Amber's suffered from nightmares since she came here. I'm not going to sit back and let an opportunity go by because I'm afraid of stepping on someone's toes. I'll go to the hospital."

Scott set the tuna salad on the plate and caught her hand in his. "Kate, I know the child means a lot to you. She's a cute little thing, and I can understand how you've gotten caught up in—"

"You'll never understand, Scott. You're not a mother." She bit back the words, but it was too late.

He pinned her with his look. "And neither are you."

She faltered for a response. "But I could be." A long ragged breath heaved from her chest.

"That's true." He squeezed her fingers, then placed his free palm over her hand. "I'm not fighting you, Kate. Don't get on the defensive with me. I'm saying that I can see why this child has captured your heart. She's so like you in many ways. Even your coloring is similar. Your eyes and hair."

Kate shook her head, wanting to halt his line of thinking. Amber might resemble her, but she wasn't Kate's child. Kate's daughter was eighteen now and lived with two loving parents somewhere in the world that Kate didn't know. The ache pressed against her heart.

Scott caught her fingers in his. "Kate, what did I say? I upset you so often without knowing why. Please, tell me. Let me into that mind of yours. You're so important to me, yet you push me away."

"Please don't. It's nothing. I know Amber means too much to me. I suppose I see the same fear in her eyes that I felt as a child. I relate to her. Don't ask why."

He drew his hand away and fell back against the chair. "I'd like to help you. I really would."

Frustration and fear slithered up Kate's back, and she narrowed her eyes. "I asked for your help once, Scott. You said no. I won't ask again."

A look of bewilderment skittered across his face, then vanished. "You mean the grandmother's records?" His voice lifted. "I haven't had a chance to tell you. I've heard rumors that my next service will be in medical. That means I'll be near the stroke unit."

His enthusiasm riled her. Why hadn't he been as eager when she first asked? Why was he so... Kate slammed the lid on her thoughts. She wasn't angry at Scott. She was angry at herself. He didn't realize the memories he dredged up. How could she blame him?

She leaned back, seeking his face, but he looked down, his index finger drawing circles on the table-top.

"I'm sorry, Scott. You touched a tender spot. I

know I've gone overboard with Amber. I'll hurt her with too much affection, and I'll feel lost when she goes back to her grandma.''

"That's what I meant, Kate. You have a mother's heart. You're tender, caring and devoted. I don't know how you deal with all that compassion.''

Kate drew her hands together on the table and knotted her fingers. "Did you go to Sunday school, Scott?''

"Sure.''

"Me, too. And one of the most beautiful pictures that hung in our Sunday school hall was the one of Jesus gathering the little children in his arms. Have you ever seen that one?'' The image rose in her thoughts. Jesus' gentle face, his arms outstretched to children of every color, every nation, every child whether good or bad.

"Every kid's seen that one, I suppose,'' he said. "So why don't I have the same depth of compassion that you do, Kate? I've seen the picture.''

She tightened the grip on her fingers like a death knot. "That's because you had parents who doted on you. Phyllis has told me about your folks. I've met them a few times. They're warm, caring people. And whether you were adopted or not, I'm sure they loved you with all their hearts.''

"You guessed that right,'' he said, displaying his wily dimples. "So what about—''

"My parents aren't like yours. I needed Jesus' wide open arms for comfort and security. I knew Jesus loved me no matter what.'' Kate struggled to

rein the emotions that boiled in her throat and behind her eyes.

"Not all parents are like that, Scott." She'd said
far more than she wanted to say, and she prayed he
wouldn't pry.

He must have read her thoughts, because he drew
both of her hands between his and pressed them
against his lips without a word.

Kate closed her eyes, afraid that it was only a
dream. Afraid to let herself go and relish in his
touch. Afraid that if he knew everything he would
turn his back and walk away.

Passing through the revolving door, Kate har-
nessed her courage, lifted her chin, and headed
straight for the information desk.

"May I help you?" the volunteer asked.

"Stroke unit. Mrs. Yates."

The woman turned to a computer screen, hit the
keys, then nodded. "Annabel Yates?"

"Yes." Kate said, not sure what her first name
was.

"Room 614."

Kate thanked her and aimed for the first bank of
elevators. When she exited the conveyance, she followed the direction of the sixth floor signs, passed
the nursing station, and followed the hallway until
she reached the grandmother's doorway.

The room held two beds, and the number indi-
cated that Mrs. Yates was in the one near the window. Passing quietly through so as not to disturb the

sleeping patient, Kate rounded the curtain and stood back, seeing an aging face distorted by a stroke.

The older woman's eyes were closed, and Kate peered at the tubing connected to her left arm and the machine monitoring her vital signs. The woman's mouth hung open, and an oxygen tube rested beneath her nose. Her chest rose and fell in ragged breaths.

Kate stepped closer, hoping the woman would sense her presence and open her eyes, but she didn't. A rattled snore rasped from her drooping mouth. Rounding the foot of the bed, Kate slid quietly into a chair and waited.

With her face aged and twisted, the grandmother didn't resemble Amber. Kate guessed her to be sixty—not old, but aged by circumstances. Her wispy salt-and-pepper hair lay matted against the pillow. No cards or flowers sat on the nightstand or windowsill, nothing to give her an identity, nothing to show someone cared.

Restless, the woman moaned and shifted, and the muslin sheet slid from her right arm. Seeing her uncovered, Kate's heart rose to her throat and her breathing shallowed. She gaped at the woman's limb, distorted by a puckered scar, tight shiny red skin amid wrinkled flesh.

Kate rose, moved to the bedside, and scanned the woman's forearm downward to her hand. Kate's stomach knotted with the sight of her gnarled fingers, twisted by some horrible accident—a scorching heat that had scarred her as it had Amber.

What had happened? Kate longed to rouse the woman awake so they could talk. But logic rose and aborted her wild scheme. Kate backed up and lowered herself to the chair. She struggled with her thoughts as time dragged, and when she gave up and rose to leave, a nurse pulled back the curtain.

"Oh, you scared me," the nurse said, staggering backward. "I had no idea Mrs. Yates had company." She moved on quiet shoes to the IV pole and checked the bags. "She's never had company before. Are you a relative?"

"No, I'm, uh, a…I'm caring for her granddaughter," Kate said. "How is she?"

The nurse shook her head. "Not good. She sleeps most of the time. Wakes only for a moment."

"What's her prognosis?" Kate held her breath waiting for the answer.

The nurse shrugged. "You'd need to talk to the doctor."

The disappointment rattled through Kate. Her lone hope drifted out of reach. "And, I won't be able to talk with her?" The answer was obvious.

"She may hear you, but I doubt if she'll be able to answer."

"I see. Then, I suppose…" Kate edged closer to the bed. "I was wondering about this burn. Do you know how it happened?"

The nurse stepped around the bed, lifted Mrs. Yates's arm, and studied the scar. "A burn. I have no idea." She drew the blanket over the woman's arm and shoulder and tucked it beneath her, then looked at Kate. "I'm sorry."

"That's okay, I just wondered," Kate said, backing toward the exit. With longing, she gazed at the elderly woman, wanting so badly to know what happened. Anything to free Amber from her dreams.

Kate lingered in the hallway outside the room, wishing some grand plan would come to her. While standing there, she noticed the placard beside the doorway with Dr. Khodijian written in black marker. Kate tucked the information away for the future. She wished he would have stopped by. At least, he might have some specifics. Finally, she lifted her tense shoulders and stretched them back before heading toward the elevators.

The situation poked at Kate's concern and heightened her curiosity. Now, she had nowhere else to turn except Scott. She'd been determined not to ask for his help again. Yet, no matter what she did, fate brought them together. A shiver coursed through her. Or was it fate?

Chapter Eight

Scott stopped at the red traffic light and organized his thoughts for the hundredth time. He'd spent a restless night thinking about Kate, and this evening, he was determined to get things out in the open.

From the day he met her, she'd brightened his drab life—black-and-white textbooks, white doctor's coat and traditional black bag. Now, Kate colored his world with the pink flush of her cheeks, the blond shoulder-length hair that glinted in the sun, the green flecks in her eyes and the soft coral of her lips.

He sounded lovesick, and maybe he was. A few years earlier, when he'd all but dismissed time for romance, he'd met Lana. She was bright, bubbly and worldly. Raised as a Christian, he'd never known Lana's wilder lifestyle. But he'd heard college days offered opportunities to spread his wings, and he did.

Taking his nose from the books, he'd puffed on a cigarette and tried liquor, then tossed those experiences aside. That wasn't for him. But Lana was soft, tempting, and willing. He'd longed to accept her offer and make love to her. But he couldn't. Not only his parents' voice rose in his head, but God's Word. And when Lana betrayed him—hurt him so deeply—he'd all but given up on women again. Until Kate.

And now that he'd loosened the fetters that bound his emotions, Kate had pulled away. But he wasn't a fool. Though she denied it, part of her cared about him. He was positive. But something inside her—fear or uncertainty—held her back. Tonight he wanted to offer her a solution to their problem.

Pulling into Kate's driveway, he turned off the ignition and sat without moving. On the spring day he first came to Kate's house, the sunshine filled the air with the scent of lilacs as he sat with Kate on the glider in the backyard.

Today, browned leaves had settled into dried, papery piles along the fences and on the ground. The autumn breeze smelled earthy—a blend of moist soil and decomposing foliage. Much had changed since that first day. Including himself.

Scott opened the car door and headed toward the house. Though only six o'clock, the sun had already lowered on the horizon, sending streaks of purple and gold against the graying clouds. He hoped Phyllis was out for the evening so he and Kate could talk privately. Maybe then, he could lift the weight from his chest.

Before he knocked, Kate opened the door. Though she smiled, he saw the hesitant look in her eyes.

"Why were you sitting in the car?" she asked.

"Daydreaming," he said, pushing the door closed. "I was thinking about the first time I came here. It was spring. Hard to believe, it's already the middle of October."

She looked at him curiously. "Time flies,"

An appetizing aroma drifted from the kitchen.

"What smells so good?" Scott asked.

"Beef stroganoff. Do you like it?"

"I'm sure I will. But I invited you to dinner."

"I felt like cooking."

Scott shrugged and quickly tucked his concerns away until later. No sense in messing up the meal if things didn't go well. His chest tightened with the possibility.

Kate beckoned him into the kitchen, speaking over her shoulder. "Phyllis is out with Darren, again. I think it's getting serious." She flashed him a smile.

"Sounds like it," he said, wondering if Phyllis would soon be walking down the church aisle. She and Darren had known each other a long time, and their romance had escalated in the past couple of months.

A fantasy fluttered through his thoughts. *Kate.* Would things smooth out for them? He'd prayed that the Lord would direct him, and he believed to-night he was following God's will.

Still, Scott wondered. In college he'd stepped beyond his books and medicine and was devastated by Lana's betrayal. Would Kate be any different? He prayed she was. If not, he prayed he would realize it before he was hurt again.

Scott leaned against the kitchen doorjamb, noticing the table had been set already. Kate motioned to a chair. When he sat, Kate placed a salad and a platter of rich, creamy stroganoff on noodles in front of him. Knowing that Kate had cooked for him gave him a comfortable, optimistic feeling. He hoped his intuition wasn't wrong.

After Kate asked the blessing, he dug into the meal. They ate in silence for a few moments, then Kate laid down her fork. "I went to the hospital today."

The words took a moment to settle into Scott's brain. "To see Amber's grandmother?"

She nodded. "Her arm and hand have burn scars just like Amber's."

Burns? The fact piqued his curiosity. "Did you talk? What did she say?"

"She's bad, Scott. She slept the whole time I was there. The nurse said she doesn't talk anyway."

"I was afraid of that," he said, watching the disappointment grow on her face.

"I don't know what to do, now," she said.

His spirits lifted, knowing he could help her. "Kate, it's not a rumor anymore. I know when I finish at the Haven, I'll be up on medical. I'll see what I can find out then.''

"Her doctor's name is Khodijian. Do you know him?''

"Not yet, but I will. Give me a few weeks, and I'll see what I can do.''

"I know you're trying to be helpful. But every day that passes without finding a way to help Amber kills me.''

"A couple more weeks, Kate. That's all.''

She didn't respond. Finally she picked up her fork and continued eating. Her sadness dampened Scott's appetite, and he nibbled the rest of his meal, hoping she didn't notice.

When they were finished and the dishes cleared away, Scott suggested they talk.

"About what?'' Kate asked.

"Let's grab a soda and sit outside. In a couple of weeks, it'll be too cold.''

"It's already cool.''

"Grab a jacket,'' Scott suggested, his hand on the doorknob.

Kate hesitated, then shrugged and hurried away. She returned with a lightweight jacket.

As they walked across the grass, Scott wanted to hold her hand or wrap his arm around her, but she seemed so distracted again he thought better of it.

They settled on the swing and he rested his arm across the back of the seat, as close as he could get to having her in his arms.

"Look at the sunset," Kate said. "Like an artist's palette."

It was beautiful. The purple and gold streaks he'd seen earlier had run together in shades of red, orange and lilac. "Pretty," Scott agreed.

"So, what do you want to talk about?" She turned to face him. "I hope you're not going to lecture me about Amber's grandmother."

"No lectures," he said, catching her sweeping hand in his and holding it against his knee.

She didn't pull away.

"Then about what?" she asked.

He let her question lay unanswered while he calmed his galloping heart. Finally, he responded. "About us."

Her hand beneath his fingers tensed, and bewilderment settled on her face. "I don't understand."

"Let me explain. From the day I met you, I felt you were special. You made me feel good and look at things differently. You didn't squawk when you went with me to look for apartments, and later you offered to let me stay here longer."

"I'd do that for any friend."

"But you weren't my friend, Kate. You barely knew me then. I was just Phyllis's brother. But just like you are with all people, you opened your arms and let me come in...that is until something happened."

"What happened?" A deep scowl creased her forehead.

"I don't know."

She tilted her head, staring with confusion into his face.

"That's what I want to talk about," Scott said.

Kate pulled her hand away. "I don't understand what you're saying." She pushed a lock of hair behind her ear.

"I think you do, Kate. But if you really don't, then I'll try to explain."

She lowered her head, and he suspected she did know what he meant.

"I like you a lot, Kate. You've added so much to my life. For a while, we laughed and had good times together. Then things changed. Maybe, since I moved in with Cass. You grew distant."

He reached over and titled her chin, directing her eyes to his. "You must realize it. Sometimes it's as if a fear comes over you and you pull away...not physically, but mentally or emotionally."

She turned away and shook her head. "I guess I don't want to get too involved with anyone, Scott."

"Okay. But why?"

"I don't know. I'm thirty-four and have a life and career." She shrugged. "I suppose I'm set in my ways."

"Set in your ways? You're young, Kate. I'm thirty-two and I'm willing to go off the deep end and do something different once in a while."

"Maybe that's the problem. I'm older than you. I'm two—"

A deep laugh burst from his chest. "Don't tell me that you think two years makes a difference?"

"It's not funny. Two years can make a big difference. Ten minutes can make a difference."

"What…" *Ten minutes?* He'd laugh, but the situation wasn't funny. He caught her face in his hands. "Kate, can we back up? Let's go back to when we first met. I like you…a lot. But I'm not heading anywhere that you aren't ready to go." The words caught in his chest. "Do you understand?"

"I don't know, Scott. I like you, too. I spend too much time at my job and not a lot on myself. You're special, too…and maybe I'm afraid of that. I don't want to be hurt." She tugged her fingers through her hair.

Scott drew her to his chest. "Kate, I won't hurt you. I promise." He edged her back, looking into her misted eyes. "How could I hurt you? I want to be your friend. Your closest friend."

Tears rimmed her eyes, and Scott's heart twisted with the emotion he saw in her face.

"You're too good for me, Scott," she said.

"I'm what? No one is too good for you, Kate. No one. Look at you. You give your life for everyone, but yourself. I see the love you have for Amber. You're doing everything you can to help that little girl. You're so full of compassion and love for everyone." He hesitated, wondering how far he could go. "And you're a beautiful woman…inside and out."

Tears rolled down her cheeks, and without hesitation, Scott leaned down and kissed the moisture that ran in trails down her face. He pressed his lips to her cheek and kissed her eyes, then touched his lips to her mouth, tasting the salty droplets.

Her body trembled against him, and Scott longed to know what secret lay hidden so deeply in her heart that she couldn't release it—speak it so it would fly away on the evening breeze.

Resting his head against her soft hair, he breathed in the fruity scent of her shampoo. She felt small and fragile in his arms. And he didn't speak, letting the emotion wash away with the tender moment.

"I'm sorry," Kate whispered against his chest. "I guess I'm feeling sorry for myself."

"You shouldn't. You should feel sorry for me because I need a friend…and you're holding back." He lightened his tone, hoping she'd relax and find the humor in his words.

She tilted her head back and looked at him. "I need a friend, too."

"Then," Scott said, his voice lilting with mimicry, "won't you be my friend?"

"I will," she said, a grin pulling at her lips. "How can I say no to that?"

Finally, Scott did what he'd wanted to do all evening. He wrapped his arm around her shoulders and nestled her to his side. When Kate laid her head against his arm, the weight that had pressed against his chest lifted and spiraled toward heaven. He looked up at the darkened sky and followed the north star to the big dipper. His heart felt as full, and he smiled, thinking his cup runneth over.

* * *

Kate stood back, resting on the leaf rake, and watched Scott. HELP couldn't have had a nicer Saturday to do the seniors' lawns, and she couldn't have been happier when Scott said he had Saturday free.

The talk they'd had a week earlier sat haphazardly in her thoughts. She struggled continually with her deep fears, pushing them away, so she could be Scott's friend. That had been their deal. Friendship. Nothing more, nothing less. Still her own heart sensed more than friendship.

The talk and the actions that night didn't mesh. He talked friends, yet she could not forget his tenderness. His gentle kisses that washed away her tears. And she thanked God he didn't ask her why she cried. Instead, he offered her his shoulder. And he promised he would never hurt her. She could ask for no more.

Turning from her thoughts, Kate grinned, watching Scott tug at the rake. Since they'd arrived at the senior's home, Mr. Brooks had latched on to him, and now as Scott tried to rake, the elderly gentleman bent his ear, following him along with sage words and nostalgic tales.

The man's loneliness shivered through Kate's mind. So often, she had felt loneliness creep up her back and tie her in knots of solitude. But since their talk, Scott's warm smile loosened the tangles.

Lifting the rake, Kate dragged the leaves through the grass to the large pile along the street in front of the house. When she turned, Scott's despondent gaze told her he needed help with Mr. Brooks. Hiding her smile, she ambled across the grass. "How are you doing?" she asked, giving the older man a smile.

"He's doin' pretty good, missy," Mr. Brooks answered in Scott's stead. "I just told him you'd be a pretty good catch."

"You did?" Kate's curiosity awakened. "And what did he say?" She caught Scott's wry grin as he sidled away.

"He said you were too slippery to get caught. Is that right?" He grinned at her with bare gums.

"He's probably right," she said, unable to draw her eyes from his toothless smile.

The man edged toward Kate as Scott made his escape.

"He's a good-lookin' fella," Mr. Brooks said. "And a strong one, too. I wouldn't wait too long, missy. There's a lot of fish in the sea, but not too many like that young fella."

She laughed, but didn't respond. Instead, she clutched the rake and pulled away the leaves caught on the fence.

Finally Mr. Brooks wandered across the grass, but his words stayed with Kate. Scott was everything the man had said. What would she do if one day he introduced her to a lovely young nurse or an attractive woman that he'd met somewhere? Could she bear it? She yanked the rake through the leaves while the possibility tugged at her heart.

Chapter Nine

Scott marveled at the crowd filling the church's fellowship hall. The area was decorated with a harvest motif of pumpkins, bushels of apples, and bunches of cornstalks. The event was Pastor Ray's thank you to the HELP group for their efforts throughout the summer.

Scott grinned, recognizing the pastor's keen public relations know-how. Besides the church's volunteers, he'd also invited the senior citizens of the community. Scanning the hall's white-haired guests, Scott eyed the talkative Mr. Brooks and dodged him, fearing he'd be cornered for the night. But guilt marched into his conscience, and Scott knew he'd relent before the night was over. Something about the older man pulled Scott's compassion out of hiding.

The church's youth had been rallied to work at

the celebration. Dressed like farmers in jeans, plaid shirts, and straw hats, the teen's chatter and good cheer raised the noise level. Looking for Kate, Scott finally caught sight of her beside a screen emblazoned with the sign, Go Fishing. Kate stood near the front of the line with a couple of elderly ladies that Scott recognized from the last Saturday of leaf raking.

Passing groups playing comical, devised games like Pin the Tail on the Plow Horse and Drop the Carrot in the Mason Jar, Scott ambled to Kate's side. "Good evening, ladies," he said, smiling at the three women.

"Want to fish?" Kate asked, gesturing to the six-foot screen decorated with colorful paper fish. "We'll give you cuts."

The ladies nodded, but he declined and grinned as Kate cast the bamboo pole, looping her line over the tall barricade. In a moment, her pole bent with a tug and she pulled in her catch. On the end of her hook was a cellophane bag of Gummi Worms. She laughed when she latched onto her prize.

"Not quite what you expected," Scott said, drawing her away from the game.

Kate opened the package and dangled a yellow-and-orange candy worm above his nose. He tilted backward and snapped at it until she let go.

A manly chuckle met Scott's ears, and he turned to face the young clergyman. The worm hung from between Scott's teeth.

Pastor Ray clasped a hand on Kate's shoulder. "If

you caught this fishing,'' he said, gesturing to Scott, ''you caught yourself a big one. Almost a six-footer, I'd guess.''

Kate laughed and Scott sucked the sticky candy into his mouth with an embarrassed grin.

The pastor's face grew serious. ''I'm glad I found the two of you together,'' he said. ''I heard from one of the church elders that Mrs. Finkell is doing okay, thanks to you.'' He looked at Scott. ''She was diagnosed with diabetes as you suspected. A few more months without treatment could have been deadly.''

''I'm so glad she's okay,'' Kate replied. ''Scott bugged me about her for a couple of weeks before I called you.''

The pastor extended his hand to Scott. ''Thanks. Having a doctor on our HELP team is a godsend. Never hesitate when you're concerned. All I do is call one of the agencies and someone drops by to check things out. You saved the woman's life.''

He patted Scott on the back and moved off to another group.

''I'm sorry I didn't listen to you,'' Kate said.

''When did you ever listen to me?'' Scott countered and gave her a wink. Yet the blood coursed through his veins, thinking of saving a life. What could be more important than his career?

''I listen,'' Kate said. ''But I'll listen more carefully next time. I promise.'' She gave him an innocent smile, then gestured toward the food counter, ''Hungry?''

He eyed the chafing dish of steamed hot dogs, the boxes of doughnuts, and jugs of cider. "Let's wait awhile. Do you mind?" His stomach egged him to consider a steak and baked potato.

"Okay, but keep in mind I'm ready any time." She took his arm and urged him across the floor to where a few courageous souls were bobbing for apples.

"Let's take a turn," she said, pulling him toward the group gathered around the large metal tub.

"No way. But I'll be your cheerleader," Scott said.

Kate rolled her eyes and edged forward, joining the group of young and old around the container and laughing at the dripping teenager with a bright-red apple clutched in his teeth.

Scott lagged back, not wanting to douse himself. Concentrating on Kate, he jumped when a hand clamped over his shoulder. He pivoted and faced a toothed Mr. Brooks.

"Howdy there, young fella," the man said. "Looks like that pretty girl of yours is havin' fun."

Scott nodded, keeping the conversation to a minimum.

"You know, when I look at young couples like you and her, I wonder where my head was so many years back."

Couple? Scott looked at Kate. That's not exactly what they were...but then what were they? Dropping his question and curious about Brooks's statement, Scott focused on the man. "What do you mean?"

"Back when I was your age, I thought my work was more important than everything else—family, friends, wife, children."

"What did you do back then?"

"Engineering. I worked for the auto industry. Cars. Tanks during the war. Thought seein' those vehicles come off the line and knowin' I played a part made me feel good," the older man said. "I figured my life was full. Didn't need a doggone thing. But I was dead wrong."

Scott's spine stiffened. Maybe engineering wasn't a worthy career, but being a physician was. If Scott had nothing else in life, he'd know that he'd helped families live healthier, happier existences.

"What do you do for a livin'?" Brooks asked.

"A physician. I'm a resident at County General."

"Now that's a career you can be proud of. But that's not all there is. I hope you know that."

"I'll begin my own practice...eventually," Scott added, defensiveness tightening his shoulders.

"Your own practice? Now that's good." The older man pulled the spectacles from his nose and drew out a handkerchief from his back pocket. As he cleaned the lenses, he pointed an elbow toward the group gathered around the apple bobbers. "Now, there's something worth hanging on to."

Scott spotted a gray-haired gentleman rising from the floor, water dripping from his face and an apple in his teeth. Then Kate knelt down and gathered her hair in her left hand, smiling at the cheering crowd around her.

"Her," Brooks said. "That's what's important. Not jobs, not money, not a mansion or a fancy car. A lovely young woman that commits to you." He turned and locked his eyes to Scott's. "Now, that's important. One that gives you a family, son."

A knot twisted in Scott's gut. "You have no family?"

"Never did. Like I said, I thought the sun rose and fell on my work. I fooled around a little, I hate to admit, but I didn't have time for marriage and children. And you know what I got to show for it?"

Scott's pulse skipped, watching that same sadness that tugged at his heart rise again in the elderly man's eyes. "I—I'm not sure, sir."

"Nothin'. Nothin' but loneliness. None of those things mean a tiddly wink to a loving family." He held his arms out shoulders height. "And look at me now. Too old for that. I have no children to leave all that money I invested. I have no wife to cuddle and share my memories on those long quiet nights. I have nothin', son."

A lump rose in Scott's throat as he watched the older man's eyes mist. "You have a point. When you're young it's easy to forget the later years." But Brooks's words cut through his blindness, like a sharp knife.

"Young people don't usually think that far. Oh, sure, they put a few bucks in some financial planner's hands. They think ahead that much. But not about things that count. Now, you on the other hand, you've got that lovely young lady there.''

"Kate's a great friend," Scott said, not sure what else to say.

"I've seen her working with this church for the past few years, and you know what I see?" He didn't pause for an answer. "I see an honest, kind and beautiful woman."

He nudged Scott's ribs. "And these old eyes can see she loves you. If you don't grab her while the gettin's good, someone else will."

Honest, kind and beautiful. Yes, Kate had all those great attributes, but Scott lingered on only one phrase. *She loves you.* Was Brooks right? Scott sensed Kate cared for him. But love? Love so evident Brooks could see it?

Scott turned and watched Kate dry her dripping face with a terry towel. Her laughter drifted to his ears, and his body warmed at the sound. She looked at him, her smile opening like a dewy morning glory, her face radiating like the sun. Scott's heart tripped and tumbled.

Kate dropped the towel into a container and walked toward him with a wave.

"Here she comes," Brooks said, motioning back.

Kate put the apple between her lips, near enough for Scott to hear the snap of the skin and to see a fine mist of juice spray into the air. "Time to feed me," she said with a playful whimper, then chewed and swallowed the bite.

Brooks gave her a friendly wink and wrapped his

arm around Kate's shoulder. "I was telling this young man that if he didn't take good care of you, someone else will. Makes me sorry I'm so old."

Kate slipped from his arm with an amiable pat on his shoulder. "I don't need to be taken care of, Mr. Brooks. I think it's you men who need looking after." She flashed a teasing grin.

Scott watched Brooks's smile sag. "You're more truthful than you know, young lady." He squeezed her arm and walked away.

Kate hesitated, then caught Scott's hand. "What was that all about?"

"Nothing," Scott said, knowing it was everything.

Chapter Ten

Kate stared at Amber's drawing lying on her office desk. Before today, she'd made no progress with the child, and despite Scott's offer to help when he moved to the medical unit, he had yet to be reassigned. She'd learned nothing new. Kate felt as if she were walking backward.

She'd used the stuffed animals, building blocks and telling stories, but Amber recalled nothing of her past—only a dog named Sparky. Today, out of frustration, Kate recalled something Scott had suggested months earlier about association. While searching through a bottom desk drawer, she stumbled across a box of colored markers and wondered what a drawing might accomplish.

When Amber arrived for her appointment, they had sat together drawing people, animals, landscapes. Not until Kate began drawing her house did things change.

Amber leaned nearer, resting her elbow beside Kate's and watched intently. After a few moments, she picked up a black marker and drew a building of her own. But instead of drawing a small bungalow, Amber's drawing was a tall rectangle, more like an apartment or office building. Then, she outlined a window in the lower portion, filling it in with black. The top square she colored in a bright red that spilled beyond her black marker boundaries.

Kate speculated its meaning: day and night, light and dark, happy and sad. When she asked Amber why she'd used those colors, the child replied, "I want it that way." Yet, the look on the child's face sent a shiver down Kate's back.

After Amber left, Kate stared at the picture, putting the pieces together, and added a new conjecture: smoke and flames. Could it be? Had Amber and her grandmother lived together back then and survived an apartment fire? She closed her eyes and bit her lower lip, grasping at fragments of the puzzle.

"Something wrong?"

Kate's eyes flew open, hearing Scott's voice. "Thinking," she said, then turned the picture around to face him. "Amber drew this today. What do you make of it?"

He ambled into the room, a hand tucked in his trouser pocket, his lab coat unbuttoned. He stood back and eyed the picture from a yard away. "Well, I'd say the windows don't look very happy." He leaned over it, looking more closely. "She didn't stay in the lines up there," he said, pointing to the upper window. "She got carried away with the red marker."

He gave Kate a grin, but she didn't smile. Instead she surveyed the drawing.

Scott scowled. "What do you think?" he asked, looking from the drawing to Kate's face.

Explaining her earlier deliberation, she added her resent speculation. "What about smoke and fire?" She punched her finger against the red color in the drawing.

He snatched the picture from the desk, studying it more carefully. "Looks like an apartment or office complex, maybe. It could be fire. What did Amber say?"

Kate repeated Amber's comment, then shrugged. "I don't know, but I hope I can get more from her. Whatever happened, she was young, I'd guess."

Scott sank into the chair that Amber usually occupied. "We should know soon."

Kate tilted her head. "Why?"

"Good news," he said with a faded grin. "Good and not so good."

"Tell me." Noting the shifting emotion in his face, Kate's breathing shallowed. "Is something wrong?"

"Barlow's coming back next week. That means I'll be full-time again at County General...at least for now. But I've been reassigned to the medical unit Sixth floor."

"Annabel Yates is on the sixth floor." She lifted her eyes to his.

"I know. That was the good part. The not so good is I won't be here with you."

Though she would miss his pop-in visits, Kate clung to his first statement. *The sixth floor.* Kate sank into the chair near him, knowing she'd allowed an intervening stretch of silence. "I'll miss you," she said.

But Scott reacted as if she'd said this as an afterthought.

He leaned forward, elbows on knees. "Next Thursday's Thanksgiving," he said.

He'd caught Kate off guard. She had anticipated a comment about her delayed response. The topic shift confounded her and she weighed the meaning. *Thanksgiving?* "Are you working?"

"No, I'm off, by some miracle. I'd like you to come to my folks' house for dinner."

Maybe it shouldn't have, but the invitation rattled her. Her first question was why? She'd met his parents when she stopped there with Phyllis, but this invitation wasn't from Phyllis. It was from Scott. The ramifications bothered her. Struggling to find a response, she faltered.

"You've already made plans," Scott said, his disappointment apparent.

"No, it's not that." She averted his scrutiny.

"Then, what is it?"

"I just wonder...well, holidays are personal times for families." She inched her gaze upward and shrugged. "I—I don't think I'd be comfortable."

"I can fix that. I'll have my folks adopt you."

His attempt at humor bounced off her like a cement block. *Adopt.* The word whacked her between the eyes and her protective shield rose between them. Accepting his invitation was too... She couldn't find the word. "Your folks will assume we're, well, serious, maybe."

His jaw sagged.

"I mean," she continued, "they'll think we have a commitment. I don't want to mislead them."

He rose and stood over her. "Kate, what's wrong? My folks will think you're my friend...and Phyllis's friend. Nothing more." With his thumb and finger, he tilted her chin upward. "And would their wondering about us be so terrible?"

Yes shot into her mind. Yes, because she could never allow herself to love Scott...and she wanted to so badly. "It's not true, that's all."

He stepped backward, his face pinched and dark. "I've invited you, Kate. I hope you'll come." He shrugged, then dropped his shoulders with a weighted sigh. "We can talk about it later."

He spun on his heel and, without looking back, stepped through the office doorway.

A blast of air shot from Kate like a punctured balloon. Why had she acted so ungrateful? Now, she'd spend Thanksgiving alone. And really, she enjoyed his family. They had always been kind. So why was she afraid?

She wrestled with her reasoning. If Phyllis had invited her, she'd have accepted without a thought.

But Scott made it different. Why? Because he was a threat. A threat to her secret. Her shame. Her guilt.

What would he do if he knew about her baby? Turn his back and walk away? She was positive he would. Any decent man would…or end up throwing it in her face eventually. And even if he didn't turn his back, his parents would certainly think she was an unfit woman for their son.

Their son? Adopted son. But that made no difference. Scott might be an adopted child, but he was loved as much as their birth daughter, Phyllis. She'd heard that from Phyllis, and she'd seen it in action. How could a fallen woman fit into the life of a man as moral and perfect as Scott?

She rose, grasped Amber's drawing from the edge of the desk, and dragged herself around the corner of her desk chair. Her back felt tense and her shoulders ached. She slid into the seat and scanned her office, remembering a time when the room gave her a sense of purpose and a feeling of success.

Lately things had changed. The colors seemed drab, the pale walls like a prison, the furniture worn and marred…like she felt. Would she ever feel whole again?

Pulling her gaze from the room, Kate refocused on the picture. Her thoughts bounced from Amber's plight to her own. If she had no other plans for Thanksgiving, what logical reason could she give Scott if she refused? He'd probe and question until she'd want to scream. She had to accept. But she'd make it very clear that they were only friends. Now and always. Only friends.

Scott gazed across his parents' dining room table at Kate. The woman amazed him. Confused him. Discouraged him. She was a jigsaw puzzle. So many pieces looked the same and each time he tried to make a match, the piece didn't fit no matter which way he turned it.

Earlier, when he picked her up at the house, she was distracted. She smiled, but he witnessed the tension in her jaw and the tight clamp of her even white teeth. Her smile was fabricated, painted on like a clown's.

With each new struggle, he questioned what it was he saw in Kate. Beautiful, she was. But lots of women were attractive, some even more beautiful than Kate. No, it wasn't beauty, but the woman herself.

His attraction was her tenderness and sincerity. And most of all, her vulnerability. Maybe it was his doctor's sensitivity to people's pain or the need to heal, but she had tangled around his heart. Each time he saw fear or regret fill her eyes, the emotion knotted in his chest until he could barely breathe.

He'd prayed, talked to God often about what he could do to make things better. But Kate gave him so little to go on. Only a bad relationship with her sister...and her parents, too. But why? When she let herself go, Kate was delightful—fun, compassionate, intelligent and determined. He saw that trait in her desire to help Amber. Why wasn't she as determined to help herself?

And today, he had to let her down again. His news wasn't good, and he'd tossed it around in his head like a fresh-from-the-oven baked potato. Too hot to hang on to, yet not the right time to lay it on the table. She'd counted on him for so long, and he had nothing to give her.

"Potatoes, Scott."

He lifted his eyes and caught his mother's strange expression.

"I asked you to please pass the potatoes," she repeated.

"I'm sorry." He lifted the dish and moved it across the table, pushing away his thoughts and latching onto the conversation.

"Scott tells us your parents live out of state," his mother said to Kate.

Kate's face shifted to a fleeting look of discomfort, then back to her strained smile. "Yes, Florida. My sister's in New York."

"Is your sister single, too?" his mother asked.

Kate flinched with the question. "I believe she is...now."

"Oh?" His mother lifted her brow in question.

"She's recently divorced, I think."

"What a pity!" his mother responded.

Listening to the dialogue, Scott ached, watching Kate's distress. Her qualified answers filled him with curiosity. Was Kate's family that estranged to make her so uncertain? His mind whirred at topics to pull his mother away from her kindly inquisition.

"I've told you about all the work we do at Phyllis and Kate's church, haven't I?" Scott said, knowing they knew, but hoping his ploy worked.

"Sounds like a wonderful congregation," his father said. "Since Phyllis got involved, I've been dropping a bee in our pastor's ear. This community could use a group like that. Now what was it called?"

"HELP," Phyllis, Scott and Kate rang out together. Their chuckle took the edge off the growing tension.

Kate continued, "'Helping the Elderly Live Proudly' is what it means."

Sitting in his parents' dining room, Scott's awareness drifted from Kate to his parents' elegant decor. Kate fit in with the rich, polished mahogany table and china cabinet filled with heirlooms and antique platters that his mother collected. Like the room, Kate seemed like a rare curio, more delicate and fragile than many of the modern, liberated women with whom he worked.

He wasn't against being liberated, and he believed women were as capable and worthy as men, but somewhere along the line, too often "liberated" had lost sight of tradition and old-fashioned values that Scott admired. Kate still embodied those traits.

As Kate chatted on relating her experiences and tales about the HELP group, she grew more animated and less tense. Scott relaxed, too, hoping he could steer the conversation back to neutral ground if his mother headed off into unsafe territory again.

But Scott's own mind was swamped with questions. He'd tried to press Phyllis for information, but she either covered up well or didn't seem to notice Kate's occasional tense withdrawal. Or maybe it was only Scott who triggered her negative reaction. Would Kate ever trust him enough to share her deep wound? And if not, should he let the relationship fly away before he was hurt again?

Thinking back to his limited experience, he seemed to have bad luck with females. A bookworm in high school, he'd dated a little, but the girls seemed to be looking for someone more adventuresome. In college, he'd buried his nose in his career, except for Lana.

And now he'd found Kate, and he'd thought she'd be different. Being a Christian, he assumed they would think alike, share the same morals and values, and flow together like two mountain streams. Instead, they seemed more like the St. Mary's River in Michigan's upper peninsula, dropping twenty-one feet from Lake Superior to Lake Huron in a tumult of white-water rapids.

But like the St. Mary's River, innovative people built locks to make passage down the river possible. What steps could he take to build a stronger, more trusting relationship with Kate? He'd prodded her once to trust him. She still didn't. But he had hopes. Maybe if she found their relationship a sure, safe haven, she'd open her heart. But he couldn't do it alone. Lately, he'd bent God's ear for direction.

When Scott tuned into the family conversation, it had shifted to Kate's work at Children's Haven. He eased against the chair, listening to his mother barrage Kate with questions about being a social worker. This time, Kate answered with confidence, filling in details and his mother's face was as animated as Kate's as she listened.

After the meal ended and the cleanup completed, they settled in the living room. His dad pulled out the family's favorite board game, and they gathered around. Between moves, they joked and chatted on safe, general topics of conversation. When the game ended, his mother protested a second game and suggested dessert.

Covering a relieved sigh, Kate watched the family's interaction, her tension lightened. Scott's mother had halted her friendly inquiry and his father kept the conversation headed in a variety of directions that didn't probe into her family. She was grateful.

They were warm and loving people. She understood why Phyllis and Scott behaved as they did, and why they cared so much for each other. They embodied what Kate thought was a true Christian family.

Yet, as the deliberation rippled through her mind, a longing slid over her...and the usual guilt. Why wasn't her family open and forgiving? They were Christians, too, but their faith was bound up in rules and self-pride. Somehow, the Lord's grace and forgiveness slipped away beneath their murky precepts.

"Okay, who wants pie?" Mrs. Ryan asked as she rose from the game table.

Hands rose, including both of Phyllis's, and they laughed.

"You want two pieces?" her mother asked.

Phyllis laughed. "Darren said he'd come by for dessert. He should be here any minute." She rose. "Let me help you, Mom."

Kate caught her arm. "No, please. You helped earlier. It's my turn."

Without a struggle, Phyllis returned to her seat, and Kate followed Scott's mother to the kitchen.

The room was as charming as the rest of the house, a blend of modern conveniences and trusty antiques. Mrs. Ryan pulled out a tray and loaded plates and cups while Kate whipped the cream.

When she finished, the older woman rested her hand on Kate's arm and grinned. "I was hoping we'd have some time to talk privately."

Panic spilled down Kate's arms and stopped at her trembling knees. Her mouth dried and words clotted in her throat.

"Sit," Mrs. Ryan said, patting the wood of a sturdy ladder back chair.

Kate caved into the cane seat and searched for her voice.

Scott's mother sat beside her, a gentle smile on her face. Grasping the server, she sliced pie and slid portions onto the plates as she spoke. "I'm so happy

Scott and you are such good friends. I've prayed so often for him to find a nice Christian woman.'' She lifted her focus from the pie to Kate.

A prickling sensation ran up Kate's spine. ''Scott's wonderful...and a good friend. I treasure him and Phyllis, too.'' Kate hoped adding Phyllis would change the tone of the conversation.

''Yes, you two have been good companions. Phyllis says the nicest things about you. I suppose you don't want me to list all the attributes.'' She grinned and brushed a strand of her hair from her cheek with the back of her hand.

''I can do without the list,'' Kate said, forcing her voice to be lighthearted.

Mrs. Ryan chuckled. ''I don't know how serious you two are. Scott and you, I mean, but I approve of your relationship. More than approve.'' Her eyes caught Kate's and held her there. ''His father feels the same way.''

Kate let go a nervous laugh—too loud and exuberant. ''You don't really know me. I'm afraid you'd be disappointed, Mrs. Ryan.''

''Please, call me Anne,'' she said.

Kate nodded.

An amiable smile spread across Mrs. Ryan's face, then she shook her head. ''We'd never be disappointed. Scott has dropped little tidbits about you, now and then. I think he's very fond of you. Very fond.''

Kate's hand shook as she slid the pie plates onto the tray. ''I'm...fond of him, too.''

"That's good." His mother said, patting Kate's hand. "Now, I think that's about it. I'll put the coffee in a carafe, and you can carry the tray for me."

Kate nodded and rose. She drew in a deep breath, hoping to steady her hands. The woman had said nothing, really, but the impetus of her words rattled Kate's thoughts. What had Scott said about her? And what would this kindly woman think if she knew the truth?

Chapter Eleven

Driving Kate home from Thanksgiving dinner, Scott's thoughts centered on his disappointing news. The evening had gone well. Although during dessert, he noticed Kate had tensed again. He wondered what his mother had said to her in the kitchen.

When they pulled into the driveway, Scott turned off the ignition, hoping that Kate would invite him in. He hopped from the driver's seat and headed for the passenger door.

But she swung it open before he arrived. "What's up, Sir Galahad? You're not trying to impress me at this late date, are you?" She gave him a toying look. "Would you like to come in?" Her question was accompanied by a knowing grin.

Praying Phyllis was still out with Darren, Scott followed her to the door. He had the news about Amber's situation, but more than that concerned him. Inside, he slipped off his jacket and hung it on the old-fashioned coatrack in the foyer.

"Tea, coffee, soda?" she offered.

"Any hot chocolate?" he asked.

She nodded and headed for the kitchen.

He trailed after her.

"I hope my folks didn't bore you to death," Scott said, wondering if she'd let slip what had troubled her. He slid into a kitchen chair, his hands folded on the table.

"They're great people," she said, glancing over her shoulder while she rummaged through the cabinet. "They weren't at all boring."

"I'm glad. They like you, too. I can tell." He studied her, wondering if she'd respond.

"I know."

Her reply jogged through his ear and bounced back a mental question. How did she know? From their behavior, maybe, but he guessed it was more than that. "My mom cornered you in the kitchen, right?"

With her back to him, Kate mixed the chocolate powder with milk and popped the mugs into the microwave. Finally, she turned. "I'm not sure *cornered* is the right word."

"But I hit the location." He shook his head, wishing he'd thought to go to the kitchen with them. Stupid, he guessed, but it hadn't entered his mind since Kate had seemed like her old self by the time they were through with dinner. "So what did she say?"

"Just what I expected," Kate said, turning to withdraw the hot chocolate. Concentrating on the mugs, she carried them to the table, then sat across from him. "She thinks we're serious about each other...or at least, she hopes we are."

His gaze sought hers. "And that's totally out of the question?" he asked. His heart sank when he saw stress pull at her face.

"Getting serious about anyone is out of the question," she said, averting her gaze from his. She studied her fingernails, rubbing her right thumb across the pale-pink polish of her left hand.

"But why, Kate? I'm sorry my mom made you uncomfortable, but I really don't understand."

"I'm too old to change. My life is settled. I have a career and...well, the church. I guess—"

The muscles knotted in Scott's neck and his shoulders felt as rigid as a private's facing a four-star general. He felt his jaw twitch as he unclamped his teeth to speak. He'd heard her "too old" comment months earlier, but he believed it was more than that. "A month ago I said the same thing about my career," he said.

Her face tilted as if he'd piqued her interest. But she crimped her fingers into a tight fist, her uneasiness remaining.

"Talking to Mr. Brooks at the harvest party made me think. And I mean, really think." He paused, organizing his thoughts. "He has no family. Did you know that?"

Kate shook her head, her face creased with tension.

"Brooks never married. Never had time for a family and children, he told me…that is until it was too late. He thought his career was all he needed. But look at him now, Kate." He slid his hand across the table and rested it on hers. "He's a lonely old man with no one to share his memories, his treasures or his time."

"People need hobbies," she said.

"Hobbies!" His voice rose, and he drew in a calming breath to soothe the emotional slap he felt from her words.

Kate's eyes were closed as if trying to block his anger by not seeing it.

But he continued, undaunted. "We're not talking hobbies, Kate. We're talking *love* and companionship. I don't know one crocheted doily or one golf club that can take the place of love." He released her hand and fell back against the chair. Kate exasperated him. Why did he bother? Giving up on her fluttered through his thoughts. Was she worth the hurt and frustration?

The room remained silent until Kate opened her eyes. Only then did Scott see the dewy mist that clung to her lashes. His chest tightened, and he mentally answered the question without hesitation. Yes, she was worth it, because he loved her. Pure and simple.

"I'm sorry, Scott. My family isn't as close as yours. And not as love-filled as yours, either. I suppose that makes it more difficult for me to want love and companionship. No one in my life…no one to hurt me.''

Those few words pushed a seed into Scott's thoughts. Was that Kate's problem? Loving meant opening herself to hurt. If he didn't ache so much, he'd laugh. For years, he'd done the same thing himself. He'd buried the desire for female companionship, uncomfortable to share his Christian beliefs…and afraid of being rejected, again, because of them.

And despite his terrific childhood, he'd grown up with questions about rejection, wondering what his birth parents were like and wondering if he might have been more loved by them. But Kate? She was raised by birth parents. Didn't that make a difference?

"I'm sorry your childhood wasn't as happy as it should have been, Kate. Growing up, sometimes I wondered about my birth parents, but that doubt was fleeting. When I really thought about it, I knew that no one could love me more than the parents who kissed and bandaged my first scraped knee and nursed me through measles and whooping cough.''

Unclasping her fingers, Kate leaned forward on her elbows and rested her chin on her hand. She listened with the intensity of a child, seeing a new, fascinating sight. But why? Scott still didn't understand.

"I'm grateful to my birth mother for having me, but I love my parents for raising me. I always thought that if a person had both birth parents to raise him the experience would be unbelievable.''

"It depends on the parents,'' Kate said. "I don't mean to sound bitter. My parents did the best they could. They raised me to know about Jesus, but they dropped *golden* out of the golden rule. They had unbending standards, and unlike God, if you broke a law—God's or theirs—it was unforgivable.''

He wanted to ask what law she had broken. What horrible thing had she done? Or had it been numerous petty things?

"Anyway,'' she said, "you'll meet them.''

"I will?''

"I heard from my mother. She and Dad are coming here for Christmas this year. Kristin, too.''

"I'd like to meet your parents. It's nice they're coming.''

"I'm not sure it's nice. They're upset with Kristin…her divorce, I should say. They couldn't get her to fly to Florida for Christmas. She told them she wanted to come back here to visit some old friends…so they decided to fly in, too.'' She rolled her eyes, then offered a faint smile. "Lucky me.''

"No matter how you look at it,'' Scott said, "they're your parents—for better or worse, I suppose…like marriage.'' He smiled with his mouth, but his heart felt sorrowful as Kate's fleeting grin wilted to sadness. He longed to take her in his arms and show her what real love felt like.

"Maybe it's time both of us trust the Lord's guidance,'' Scott said. "In the scheme of things, it seems

God wanted the world in twos. I suppose that's why under all of our personal fears, people long for a partner. Like Mr. Brooks.''

For the first time, Kate captured his gaze. "It's not that I don't feel emotion, Scott. Maybe, I'm afraid of it. I don't want to be carried away without using my reasoning. Did you ever let your desire win over your good sense? Maybe I'm afraid I can't control my emotions.''

Her eyes filled with a mixture of emotions: fear, hurt, sorrow. Scott didn't know which.

Then, Kate lowered her head. "Maybe that's what I'm afraid of…that I'm incapable of hearing God's will when I'm so tangled in my own.''

Her words spun through Scott's puzzled mind. He speculated what she might have done in her childhood. Or maybe what she hadn't done that she should have.

The conversation sagged and he didn't know what else to say, fearing his words would only bog things down worse. Then Amber's plight nudged him again. Their present discussion hadn't gone well, and he knew the next wouldn't get any better, but he couldn't let it go any longer.

His pulse shifted into passing gear as he shuffled through words, trying to decide the best way to tell her what he'd done. Finally, he spit it out. "I didn't find anything in Mrs. Yates's records to help you.''

Kate's body stiffened, and she pulled her back from the chair. "You checked?''

"I had a chance to look yesterday…but I didn't

mention it earlier. I hated to put a damper on Thanksgiving dinner. I knew how much you hoped for something more definite.''

"Nothing? Are you sure?''

"Positive. The records stated, 'Old burn scars on right hand and forearm.'''

Kate slumped against the chair and closed her eyes.

"I'm sorry, Kate.''

She opened her eyes and stared into space. "I'm being foolish. What difference would it make if I knew what happened? I'm not sure it'll help Amber one way or the other.'' She raised her hand and pressed two fingers against her temple, rotating them in gentle circles. "But if I understood, I'd hope I might be able to—''

"I've been thinking,'' Scott said.

"Thinking?'' She dropped her hand. "About what?''

"Newspapers.''

Her disappointed face brightened, and she leaned forward.

"If a child was burned in a house or apartment fire, we should find it in the newspaper. The library keeps microfiche copies of all the periodicals. As long as it happened in the metro area, we should be able to find it.''

"It would take forever, Scott.'' Her excitement dimmed.

"Maybe not. At least, we can try.''

And even if it took forever, it would give him

more time to prove to Kate that he loved her and that he wasn't like her parents. Scott would forgive her for anything.

Through her wide front window, Kate sat on the sofa and watched a few downy snowflakes drift and twirl on the winter wind. She checked her wristwatch. Scott should arrive any minute and she prayed the heavy snowfall waited until they selected her Christmas tree.

With her family coming for the holidays, Kate had taken a couple of days off at the Haven so she could shop and decorate the house. No matter how difficult their visit would be, she promised herself to focus on Christ's birth. That would cheer her, no matter what.

Then Scott was another story. Daily, she asked herself what she was doing. Why had she allowed him to get under her skin and into her heart? If she had any gumption, she'd end it now. Now, before more pain settled into her soul and eradicated the little joy and purpose she had found in her work.

In a way, she knew how it happened. They'd called a truce of friendship. If they'd been able to stick to that agreement, things may have worked...but even then, she knew better. With the smoothness of satin, her emotions had slipped away and tangled in Scott's heartstrings.

And Scott was right about one thing. She'd allowed her past to weigh too heavily on her life. No one could rid her of the feelings, but herself...and

God. A wave of shame washed over her at her neglect. When would she accept the truth that with God all things are possible?

On her own, she'd struggled to develop a plan of action, like she would for one of her clients at the Haven. But working on someone else's problems was a million times easier than working on her own. She needed to open her heart and mind to the Lord's will.

Scott's sedan slowed and turned into the driveway, and Kate rose. She slipped on her jacket and wrapped a scarf around her throat. No matter what the day held, Kate prayed she could take each moment as it came, accepting whatever it may be. And deep inside she knew that something kept her from walking away. Sometimes, she liked to think it was really God's bidding…and not her own wishful dreams.

The doorbell sounded, and before she could move, the door opened.

"It's me," Scott called, as he stepped into the foyer. When their eyes met, a grin slid over his lips. "I'd say you're ready."

"Just need my boots," she said, sliding off her terry cloth slippers. "I'd like to get the tree before it snows any heavier." She stepped into her sturdy footwear, then bent down to tighten the laces.

"We're supposed to get three to four inches."

When Kate lifted her head, they stood face-to-face, only inches apart. Her pulse skipped as the scent of mint hovered on the air.

Scott captured her chin between his thumb and fingers. "Do I detect a smile on these lips?"

Unable to speak, she nodded, longing to have his full sweet mouth touch hers. Though her logic resisted, her heart cried out to be loved.

As if God answered her prayer, Scott lowered his cool lips and warmed them against her own. His peppermint mouth lingered tenderly while his arms drew her tightly against his icy jacket.

As if nothing mattered, Kate yielded to him. The wintery weather outside couldn't penetrate the inner warmth that rose from her knees to her heart. With amazing gentleness, Scott's lips caressed hers, and when he drew back, the radiance in his eyes melted her hidden fears.

"Now that's more like it," he said, brushing his fingers along her cheek.

Without another word, he opened the front door and herded Kate outside. Scott continued down the steps while she locked the door.

Kate hated to break the spell that snuggled lovingly in her thoughts, but once on the way, their conversation switched to Christmas and, finally, to her latest idea that she'd tossed about. Not knowing how he'd respond, she held her breath.

"I've been doing a lot of thinking about Amber. But I need your help...one more time."

He glanced her way without a word, then shifted his concentration back to the road.

She studied his face, wondering if he was upset with her request, but the telltale twitch of his jaw remained unmoved so she continued. "I was thinking that all we need is the date of the fire...that is, if we're right about a fire."

"So how can I help?"

Noting the positive ring to his voice, Kate mustered courage and plowed ahead. "You can ask someone in the hospital records department if Amber Yates has ever been admitted to County General and if she has, then ask the date."

"Don't get your hopes up, Kate. What if Amber had been admitted for asthma or something else when she was a child—"

"I know it's a long shot, but could you try?"

He flashed her a tender grin. "Sure, but don't be disappointed, okay?"

Though she nodded, Kate had to face her inability to deal with disappointment. Her success rate was zilch.

The conversation shifted back to Christmas plans, and soon, they pulled up to a large Christmas tree lot. Kate wrapped her scarf tightly around her throat and tugged on her gloves before exiting the car.

The wind had strengthened, and the snowflakes were blowing into mounds along the curbs and buildings. Scott moved beside her and caught her fingers in his as they stepped between the chain-link fence and trekked down the row of trees. With their hands united, Kate felt complete and nestled against his side as they trudged along.

The evergreens were now weighted with the snowy burden, and large snowflakes caught in

Scott's hair and the crystalized patterns sprinkled his shoulders. He slowed, then halted and grasped a tree that leaned against the fence. After shaking its branches, Scott turned and displayed the full, but squatty Scotch pine. "What do you say?" His breath lingered as a smoky cloud on the air.

She shook her head. "I don't like pines that much. I want a *real* Christmas tree."

His cheeks glowed with a rosy tint, and deep smile lines dimpled his face. "A 'real' Christmas tree? And what might that be, Katie?" His voice lilted with humor.

"I'll know it when I see it. They're different."

His face twisted in bewilderment, then brightened. He grabbed her hand, and she ran beside him to keep up with his long strides. They scooted up one row and down the other while the snow fell in heavy sheets, piling on the branches and their lashes.

Finally, Scott slid to a halt. He released her hand, eyed a pile of trees far back on the lot, lifted one, shook the branches, then faced her.

A smile pulled on her mouth as she eyed what she considered the ideal Christmas tree. "Perfect," she said, admiring the tall-reaching top spire waiting for her Victorian angel and the stair-stepped limbs with short needles, so much sparser than a pine. "Now, that's a real Christmas tree. See all of the places I can hang my special glass ornaments."

Scott drew her into his free arm, then eyed the tree. "For future reference," he said, giving her a wink, "this is a plain old balsam."

"Balsam," she repeated, feeling the prickly branches pressing against her cheek. "I like plain old things."

He let the tree drop back to the pile and nudged her around to face him. "Not me, Kate. I like charming, young things with glowing cheeks and sparkling eyes." He traced his gloved finger along her jawline, then cupped her chin in his hand. "Especially ones who like balsam Christmas trees."

Kate knew what was coming and tilted her eager mouth to meet his. No longer did Scott's sturdy physique drag out her old memories. Today, hidden from other customers by the row of evergreens and the fast-falling flakes, she clung to his broad frame. And when their icy lips touched, her entire being warmed with her hopes for Christmas and the sweetness of their growing relationship.

Chapter Twelve

Scott's brain was as tired as his body. The night shift was a killer, and the past four weeks hung on his memory like a bad dream. The only day that glowed in his mind recently was the afternoon he helped Kate buy the Christmas tree. But now, he, groaned with the long nights and even longer days when he tried to sleep.

He drew in a grateful sigh, knowing that later that day he would hear if he was headed for the afternoon shift or if he'd miraculously be reassigned to days. Shift changing was the plight of doctors doing their residency.

Kate's spirit had brightened in the past weeks. Whether it was the excitement of Christmas or their talk, Scott didn't know. And he didn't care. He enjoyed every minute of her laughter, smiles and good cheer. They'd shared warm, tender moments, and

Scott had no doubt where his heart was headed. Right into Kate's arms. His only concern now was assurance she felt the same way.

With Christmas only two weeks away, Scott had offered to help Kate put up her decorations, and he hoped to be the bearer of his own joyful tidings that day. But when he contacted the records clerk at County General, she found no reference to Amber in the hospital files. With that news, Scott felt as disappointed as he knew Kate would feel.

He hated to disappoint her again and had struggled with the problem of Amber's background. When the obvious resource slithered into his head, he wondered why Kate hadn't thought of it first.

During his hospital dinner break, he found an unused telephone and called his sister, praying she would be home...alone. Kate had mentioned she'd be out that evening doing some heavy-duty Christmas shopping.

When Phyllis answered, he explained the situation. "So I figured if anyone knew a way to access a child's records, you'd have some ideas."

Silence filled the line.

Knowing his sister, Scott waited, praying she'd offer him a possible solution.

"I'm thinking," Phyllis said. After a lengthy pause, she responded. "If Amber's drawing showed a high-rise apartment, my guess is that they lived in Detroit back then. So logic says, she'd have been treated at a city hospital."

"That's a lot of hospitals," Scott said, trying to keep the disappointment from his voice.

"Her birth record would list the hospital where she was born, and if the fire occurred when she was two or three, the family may have lived in the same area and—"

"And she would have gone to the same hospital," Scott said.

"That's seems logical," Phyllis agreed.

Scott agreed. "So where can I get a copy of her birth records?"

"You can't. Not in Michigan."

Frustration plowed through him. "Why not?"

"Birth records are restricted to family and a few legal exceptions."

Though her words were discouraging, her voice hinted that she could offer some hope. Praying he was correct, Scott asked, "And the exceptions are?"

"Legal guardians."

A smile skipped to his face. "And right now, Children's Haven is Amber's legal guardian." If Phyllis could identify Amber's birth hospital, then Scott prayed he was only one telephone call away from learning the date of the fire.

On Friday night, Kate moved the storage boxes filled with her Christmas decorations into the living room. Working at the Haven all day and preparing for the holidays at night made her more than tired. She was grateful Scott had volunteered to help.

This year, Phyllis was spending more time with

Darren, and Kate guessed her friend would be wearing an engagement ring after the holidays. Though she was happy for Phyllis, Kate felt sorry for herself. Her life would be even lonelier without her housemate's presence.

Tugging open a large cardboard box, Kate pulled out a lengthy strand of evergreen roping. Though artificial, it looked festive draped down the staircase and tied with big red bows. Having the house look perfect was important this year for her family's visit. Though she tried not to feel as she did, Kate wanted to demonstrate how successful and happy she was…even if it wasn't totally true.

Thinking of Kristin, Kate's jealousy surfaced again. Perhaps this year, her parents' frustration would be aimed at her sister and her divorce, giving Kate a breather.

Divorce was one of her parents' unforgivable sins. Though God lovingly forgave those who repented their sins, Kate reveled in the knowledge that remaining single meant divorce was one sin she would not commit. But then Scott's image appeared, setting her nerves on edge.

When reality struck her, Kate knew inviting Scott over to meet her family was the last thing she wanted. But it was the only appropriate thing she could do. She'd wrestled with a million reasons and excuses. And that's exactly what they were—excuses. Scott wouldn't understand if she avoided an introduction and neither would her parents. So again, she prayed, hoping to hand her fears over to God.

Shrugging off her worries, Kate gathered up the strand of roping and lugged it to the bottom of the staircase. She dropped it in a pile, then returned to the box. More roping lay curled in the bottom, and she pulled it out and carried the shorter piece to the mantel. Once she twisted the roping with miniature lights and set out a display of holiday candles, she knew it would create a lovely effect.

As she untangled the roping, Kate heard the door open. She spun around and paused, seeing Scott standing in the doorway with packages tucked in his arm.

"I didn't wait long enough, did I?" he said, eyeing the boxes piled on the floor.

"You'd have to wait days," she said, giddily juggling two large candles. "What's in the bags?"

"Something to set a festive mood." He placed one package on the chair and pulled a carton of eggnog from the other. "Voilà."

"Eggnog?"

"It's tradition. This and Christmas music go along with decorating. That's how I grew up."

"You had a pretty special life," she said, wanting to make a joke, but none came to mind. Often, she wondered about her own baby's life. Baby? No, not any longer. Her daughter would be eighteen now. Almost nineteen. She prayed God had guided her child to a loving, Christian family like Scott's.

He scooted to Kate's side and slid his arm around her waist. "You don't like eggnog?"

She nearly laughed at his pensive expression. "Sure. Why?"

"Because you look so serious."

Hastily, she pushed away her melancholy and veiled the truth. "I was guessing what's in the other bag."

"Ah, so that's it." He shot across the room and grabbed up the second bag. When he returned, he slipped it into her hands. "It's a little gift."

"For me?"

He nodded.

Puzzled, she opened the sack and peeked inside. A six-inch cube-shaped box sat on the bottom. She opened it and caught her breath. "It's beautiful, Scott."

Undoing the protective covering, Kate pulled out a delicate glass ornament. Its iridescence reflected a myriad of pastel hues, and gold lettering spelled out My Special Friend. Tears pushed against the backs of her eyes and ran, unbidden, down her cheeks.

Scott caught her in his arms and pressed his cheek against her wet skin. "It's not nearly as beautiful as you are, Kate."

She faced him and reveled in the tenderness that glinted in his eyes. "I love it, Scott." The words she wanted to say stuck in her throat: And I love you, too.

"I remembered when you said you liked places to hang your special ornaments. So I'm adding one to your collection.'' He tilted her chin upward and gazed at her with heavy eyelids. ''And I pray it's the first of many.''

As his mouth lowered to hers, a tremor wavered through her limbs and quivered in her chest. She came too close to losing her senses in this man's arms.

Delighting in the sensation, she clasped the back of his neck, feeling his muscles tighten, then slid her hand to the flexing strength of his shoulders. His thick arms held her captive and she surrendered to the swirling emotions.

His body trembled against hers. Then, he drew back. ''I don't think this is getting your house decorated. Not in a million years.''

She wanted to tell him she didn't care about the ornaments and bows, but instead, she flagged her flailing emotions with a heady sigh, nestling her face against his jacket and smelling the musky scent that surrounded him.

They stood still, caught in each other's arms until Kate drew back. ''How about some eggnog?'' she said.

Scott's laugh broke the silence, and she joined him, knowing she needed the humor to bring her back from the uncontrollable feelings she had experienced.

''With ice. Lots of ice,'' Scott added with a sheepish grin. He stepped away and pulled off his jacket. ''While you get the nog, I'll put on some music.''

Kate carried the carton into the kitchen and filled two glasses with the thick holiday drink. She used the time to calm her emotions and rein her thoughts. If she truly loved Scott and he loved her, she had to tell him about her past...about her child. But how could she?

No matter how much Kate's feelings grew, Scott's words pressed against her thoughts. Chastity, a gift for a spouse. When they first met, Scott's athletic physique had triggered unwanted memories about Ron. But no more. Tonight, she clung to Scott's firm, strong frame with only thoughts of him.

Kate shook her head. She would lock her fears away. Forget her horrible concern for the time being and enjoy the holiday.

She refocused on the two tumblers and breathed a sigh. As Christmas music drifted into the kitchen, Scott's pleasant baritone voice rode along on the carol. After Christmas, maybe then she could deal with her dilemma and make a sensible decision. At the moment, she had no strength to fight her feelings. She would enjoy the holiday...and revel in Scott's attentiveness.

She grabbed the two glasses, and when she returned to the living room, Scott was plowing through the cardboard boxes, a Christmas table covering draped over his shoulder like a cloak.

"Practicing to be a Magi?"

"Something like that. I do believe in miracles."

The grin on his face caused her to halt, and she

faltered, studying him for a moment. "Okay, I give. What's up?"

He tilted his head with the look of sheer innocence.

Kate marched toward him, pushing the glass of eggnog against his chest and moving him backward to the sofa. When the seat was behind him, she shoved the drink in his hand. "Now, sit, and tell me why you look like the cat who ate the canary."

She sat beside him on the edge of the cushion and rested the glass on her knee.

"What do you want to hear first?" he asked.

Anxiety sizzled along her nerve endings. "If it's something about Amber, that's what I want to hear."

He grinned and began his story, detailing the path that led him to Phyllis. "So she called the Wayne County birth records clerk and requested the birth hospital name. They gave it to her over the telephone."

Kate's heart beat so fast she felt as if she couldn't breathe. "So tell me," Kate said.

"She was born at Harper Hospital."

"Then we need to check there—"

"I already did."

Excitement reeled through Kate's body. "So stop with the suspense. What else?"

"She was admitted to Harper Hospital with burns three years ago in February, and was moved to Children's Hospital the next day."

Kate fell back against the seat cushion. "I can't believe it was that simple."

Scott chuckled. "Easy for you, maybe. You didn't do anything." He tousled her hair.

Kate retaliated, then threw her arms around his neck. "Thank you, Scott. And Phyl, too."

Scott brushed her hair from her cheek. "Remember, this is only the beginning. We still need to check the library."

"I know."

"Phyllis tried to pry a little more information out of the clerk, but the woman asked her to mail an official release of information slip, so she just thanked the clerk and hung up."

As reality shuffled through her, Kate shifted on the cushion. "If anything happens to Mrs. Yates, the Haven will need to investigate further anyway. Amber must have some family somewhere. What happened to her mother and father?"

Scott shrugged. "Hard to tell. Parents place kids for adoption. Who's to say they don't give them to relatives? Amber's parents might not want to be found. Or sadder, maybe, they died in the fire."

Kate closed her eyes, unable to face either of the possibilities. She cringed at the concept of parents not wanting their children. Though it had been best, years earlier she would have done anything to keep her baby, but the choice wasn't hers. At the age of fifteen, what kind of life could she have given the child?

"Hey, cheer up!" Scott said, jostling her back to

the present. "All we need is some time in the library and you should have your answer."

"Right," she said, jumping up from the sofa and struggling to recapture her Christmas spirit.

Scott grabbed her hand. "I almost forgot. Here's some more good news. I'm back on days starting Monday."

"Great. How did that happen?" She loved Scott working days. He'd spoiled her with his attentiveness and spur-of-the-moment invitations. The past weeks with Scott on the night shift, he slept before going to work, and the evenings dragged for Kate like they had months earlier before she knew him. Worse than dragged. Then, she hadn't realized how lonely and empty her life had been. Now, the awareness seemed overwhelming.

Her thoughts had drifted again and she missed Scott's explanation. But when one horrible phrase struck her inner ear, her breath vanished and she choked. "What? Say that again," she said, trying to regain her voice.

"Madonna House. Have you heard of it?"

Had she heard of it! Her heart slid to her toes, and she nodded a feeble yes.

"I'm working there like I did at the Haven. Three days a week."

"But you're not a gynecol—"

"No, but we do regular checkups, deal with health issues, etc. Once a month a gynecologist comes in to check on the pregnancies."

"That's so different from—" Fear rose up her

arms and pushed against her heart. What had she done? She'd almost confessed without realizing it.

Scott's puzzled eyes studied her. "Different from…?" he asked.

Her mind flew, searching for a response. Any answer than to admit that's where she had been eighteen years earlier. Gooseflesh prickled on her skin. "Different from many of those agencies. I figured they still used nurses. I knew a girl from high school who went to one of those homes."

"Ah," he said, his quizzical expression shifting to a grin. "I suppose that many years ago it was different. Times have changed. Attitudes have changed. I'd guess it's easier now."

Easier? Never. Not when you carry a child for nine months. Not when you feel the weight against your belly and feel the tiny limbs shift and kick inside you. Not when you lay on a hard table to be examined as if you were little more than a sheep…or worse. How could it be easy to never see the child who carried your blood through its tiny veins?

This time Kate caught herself drifting in thought and prayed the ache in her throbbing heart would calm. She pulled her gaze upward, unknotted her hands, and drew his attention with a sweeping gesture to the unadorned room. "If we're going to get some decorating done, we'd better get busy."

Scott captured her extended hand and drew her into an embrace. "How about slapping a bow on the banister and calling it a day. I'd rather sit on this sofa and cuddle you in my arms.''

''Don't sweet-talk me, buster. Get busy.'' Playfully, she broke loose from his arms, but her teasing had been a ploy. She tucked her trembling hands into the pockets of her jeans, praying he hadn't felt the nerves quaking in her body…and in her soul.

Chapter Thirteen

Listening to Kate's family after dinner, Scott struggled to unlock his jaw and release the tension. From the moment he arrived, Kate's well-meaning parents chopped away at both their daughters' defenses. He tried to understand, assuming they only wanted the best for their girls. Scott sorted through their comments, and his heart lifted, praising God for the Lord's unfailing forgiveness. Mr. and Mrs. Davis did not know the meaning of the word.

Meeting Kate's sister offered Scott an in-depth view of their sibling relationship. Though Scott found greater beauty in Kate, Kristin's face and figure were perfection…and Kristin, obviously, knew it. She had swung her hips, flaunted everything below her neckline and pursed her lips in what she probably thought was a seductive pose.

But Scott turned lovingly toward Kate and, emotionally, caressed the natural charm of her near-round face, creamy skin, delicate button nose and eyes that took him on a journey to her heart.

Why couldn't Kate see that her loveliness was both inside and out? Nothing in Scott's opinion could replace sincerity, honesty and selflessness. Kate had it all.

Drawing himself from his thoughts, Scott had lost the family's conversation and sorted through the snippets he'd heard.

"Kate, I know you," her mother said. "You're much too involved with those pitiful children. I wish you'd look for a job that has a good income and gives you a sense of achievement."

Tension stiffened Kate's back while her eyes narrowed and sparked. "It's people's impression of these children that's pitiful, mother, not the kids. To me, they're precious. I wish you could understand that I love my career."

With a sidelong look at Kate, Scott's reserve crumbled. "You should see Kate at the Haven," he said, unable to control the defensiveness that rose to his shoulders. "She's respected by the staff and loved by the children. These kids are victims of circumstance."

"That might be," Mr. Davis said, "but the way I look at it, the circumstance is mainly unChristian women not using their God-given sense."

"Not using birth control," Mrs. Davis muttered.

"That's not true," Kate said, her voice fading

with defeat, "but you'd have to be there to understand."

"It's difficult understanding stupidity," Mr. Davis said. "The Lord gave us *ten* commandments…not eleven or twelve. Ten clear-cut commandments. Even my own girls can't seem to follow them." His narrowed eyes focused on Kristin.

Kate's face paled, and she shriveled into the cushion.

Scott heard her father's words, but their meaning was lost. What had Kate done that was so horrible that her father dredged it out today? Struck by a possibility, Scott balked. Divorce? No, Kate couldn't have been divorced, too.

"Sorry, Dad," Kristin snapped, "I guess my *husband* didn't learn the one about coveting his neighbor's wife."

Neither of Kate's parents commented. Instead, her father turned his attention to Scott. "Now, here's a young man that a parent could be proud of." He leaned forward, balancing his elbows on his knees, his hands folded in front of him. "And you've got what I call a career," he said. "One day, the money will be rolling in."

Scott leaned forward with a chuckle. "You might think I'm naive, but I didn't become a doctor for the money. I like helping people, pure and simple. Just like Kate."

"That's very benevolent, young man." He leaned back and pulled on the end of his thin mustache. "I read the Good Book. We should all show compassion like the Lord commands, but…a little green stuff never hurt anybody.'' His lip curled in a wily grin, and he rubbed his thumb against his upturned fingers.

Scott's stomach churned at Kate's parents' lack of discernment, and he wondered how Kate turned out so warm and caring. Many times, Kate had made references to her less-than-loving childhood. He'd witnessed Kate's fear to accept peoples' approval and to trust them. How many times had she backed away from him? The more determined he was to reveal his growing feelings, the more Kate scrambled out of reach.

With a long-awaited lull in the conversation, Kate suggested dessert and headed for the kitchen. Scott trailed after her, promising himself not to make reference to any of the tension that had transpired. Kate's misery struck him as if it were his own.

When Kate realized he'd followed, she turned around. ''I can do this alone.''

''I know, but I want to help.''

She shrugged and pivoted to face the cabinets.

Scott stepped behind her and slid his arms around her shoulders, pressing his cheek to her sweet-scented hair. ''I really wanted a minute alone…to hold you in my arms.''

''Why would you want to do that?'' she asked, pulling dessert plates from the cabinet.

Scott grasped the plates from her fingers and, with his free hand, turned her to face him. He eased the china onto the counter and wrapped his arms around her waist. "Because I love you, Kate."

Astonishment leaped to her face, and her mouth sagged. Grasping his words, she shook her head as a frown furrowed her brow. "No. No, Scott, you can't love me. We made a deal."

He froze in place. "A deal?" His mind whirled backward, seeking the moment they had made a deal. "I don't remember a *deal*, Kate."

She pressed her hands against his chest, pushing him away, but he held her fast.

Her eyes pleaded. "A couple of months ago…you said 'Let's back up and start over.'"

"And we did," he said, remembering the day that was so like this one.

Her face paled, and misty tears welled in her eyes.

"We started over," he continued, "and we ended up here…in each other's arms."

Her palms pushing against his chest belied his statement. But he couldn't release her. Kate had to see the reality and learn to accept it. Neither she nor Kristin were as awful as their parents inadvertently made them feel. The Davises were confused, not knowing how to teach God's laws without forgetting God's love.

But Scott knew both and would hang on to Kate as long as he could. "Don't be afraid of me, Kate. You're already a part of me, and I can't let you go. Please, let me help you. We can deal with the past, I promise."

Her drawn face tilted upward. "I'm not the wonderful person you seem to think, Scott. You deserve a good mate, a loving woman who's pure and comp—''

"Pure?" He lifted his hand to her trembling chin, cupped it, and pressed his fingers against her lips to silence her. "You're pure as the driven snow, Kate. You're as white and guiltless as God's promise."

Her eyes widened. "I know I'm sinless in God's eyes, but I'm not in my parents'…or in yours if you knew the—''

Addled with her determined condemnation, he did what his heart desired. He silenced her with his lips, tasting the salty tears and cherry flavor of her lip gloss. She trembled against his body, and he ran his hands across her back in soothing strokes, longing to cradle her in his arms.

"My, my."

Kristin's voice cut through the tender moment, and Scott peered at her without moving.

"I wondered what was taking so long," she said, arching an eyebrow. A mocking snicker left her throat.

With Kate's face buried against Scott's chest, she furtively brushed the tears from her eyes, then slid out of his embrace and pulled the cups from the cupboard.

"My fault," Scott said, making light of the moment, "I can't resist your sister. She's like a magnet." He drew his hand across Kate's unyielding shoulder, then turned to Kristin. "Did you come to help?"

Kate's sister chuckled, again. "Doesn't look like you need any help."

"We all need help," Scott said, piling the cups onto a tray.

"What can I do?" Kristin asked as she strode across the floor toward them.

Kate gave her quick instructions, and together, they filled the tray with the Christmas china and desserts. Scott lifted the tray while Kate carried the carafe.

Sidling to Scott's side, Kristin snatched a cookie from the plate with a wink. "Mommy and Daddy are such sweeties, aren't they?" Her eyes locked with Scott's.

"They're well-meaning," Scott said and slipped passed her heading for the living room, his mind twisting and turning, hoping to decipher Kate's puzzling world.

Kate stretched out on her bedspread, her mind reviewing the holiday. Phyllis had popped in and out, spending most of her time with Darren's family, and as Kate and Scott had suspected, Phyllis's finger now boasted a beautiful diamond.

With her parents away visiting friends for the New Year and Kristin staying with an old high school girlfriend, Kate had her first quiet moment since the holiday began.

Yet, her thoughts were less than peaceful. As if providence would not let go, Scott had asked her to attend a holiday party with him at Madonna House.

Unable to find a valid reason to refuse, Kate agreed. Now, the weight of memories and fears pressed against her heart.

She trembled, wondering how she could return to the place where she'd stayed like a prisoner for nearly six months. The name alone, Madonna House, wrenched through her, tearing away the years that cushioned the miserable memories and shame of her stay there, hiding her growing truth from the world.

No doubt time had changed the facility and improved—if that was possible—a pregnant girl's stay. Never during her residency had there been a holiday or occasion celebrated with a party, especially one that included a doctor.

Her darkest recollections hinged on the faces of the unknown men in white coats who treated her with animosity and degradation. She never saw the same physician twice, and none of them had prepared her for the pain of childbirth or the sorrow of releasing her unseen baby for adoption.

The frightened occupants' main source of care was a few nurses who soothed them with good-meaning words that still tore at her very fiber. "You'll have another baby some day. Just wipe this whole thing from your thoughts," and "You don't want to shame your family, do you? We'll find your baby a good home."

Like opening a wound, other festering words oozed from her mind. "You're selfish, not thinking of your child." "You can't take care of a baby."

Though their words bore the truth, they had pierced Kate's self-esteem just as her parents' shame had knifed through her guilt-filled conscience.

Tonight, she had to face both Madonna House and Scott. With her family's presence, he hadn't questioned her parents' numerous innuendos and inflexible thinking. Knowing Scott, Kate had no doubt he would ask eventually. And she was too weary to contrive an answer.

All this had happened on the heels of Kristin's visit. Her sister's presence had wedged its way into Kate's old insecurities. Kate viewed her sister's blatant flirtation with Scott and shriveled, feeling less appealing and less worthy. And why? Scott said nothing, no reference to Kristin's beauty or behavior. Zero.

With the time drawing nearer, she pulled herself up from the coverlet, and after studying the clothes in her closet, she tugged out a muted-green knit ensemble. Kate stepped into her skirt, then tugged the long tunic over her head. The garment discretely covered her slender frame, and best of all, the color and style allowed her to hide beneath its simple design.

The gold necklace Scott had given her for Christmas lay on the dresser, a series of golden beads interspersed with pearls. Though the chain was beautiful, her mother's adage marched through her thoughts. "For every pearl a woman wears, she will cry a hundred tears." Inspecting the lovely beads,

Kate assessed that she had already cried her share for every pearl that adorned Scott's lovely gift.

At the bathroom mirror, she highlighted her cheeks with blush and her eyes with shadow, and she brightened her mouth with a lush coral shade. Looking at her straight hair, she caught it back in a gold hair clip and added pearl studs to her earlobes.

As she snapped off the light, Scott's voice sailed down the hallway. He met her halfway, and when he saw her, he stopped—and so did her heart. Tonight, his broad shoulders and chest were bound beneath a hunter-green mock-turtleneck with a beige-flecked wool sport coat. His good looks amazed her, and as he drew her into his arms, she remembered to breathe.

"Is this new?" Scott asked. "You look great."

"No, it's been hanging in my closet. It's too dressy for work."

His finger traced the drape of the gold-and-pearl beads, then lifted his hand up to her shoulder. "The necklace looks nice. And your hair…you don't wear it up often. I like it." His last words were a murmur as he bent down and pressed his lips to the unprotected curve of her neck.

An electric tingle shot down her arm and settled in her solar plexus. Protecting her sensitive skin to his touch, she pressed her ear to her shoulder.

He didn't linger, but wrapped his arm around her and walked beside her to the foyer closet. When she had slipped on her coat, Scott opened the door and a cold blast of air swirled around her ankles, sending chills down her arms. As she stepped to the porch, cold, anxious fear shivered down her spine like a criminal taking his last steps to the gas chamber.

Standing beside Kate at the table covered with a holiday paper cloth, Scott surveyed the dishes filled with simple appetizers and Christmas cookies. While they visited and munched on snacks, a few parents arrived and another physician from the hospital.

Scott took in the surroundings. Shy, plain-faced girls clustered in small groups at one end of the room, their bulging tummies pressed against lacy maternity tops while noisier teens, their eyes outlined with black kohl and lips highlighted with dark color, bounced to the cassette player's rhythmic beat. These girls were dressed in clinging T-shirts with phrases, like Baby emblazoned above a bright-yellow arrow pointing to the telltale protrusion.

Though Kate had hesitated accepting the invitation, she'd been a good sport. When he arrived, she had looked so lovely…and fragile.

Stepping into Madonna House, Scott had noticed Kate's curious expression as she scanned the large, unadorned living room and glimpsed into the open doorways. He suspected she was thinking of the needy children she worked with daily at the Haven. Kate's heart was undauntedly tender.

Speaking at length with the housemother and a nurse, Kate had learned about the facility, and Scott noticed her withdraw for a brief moment like she did with her parents. He hadn't spoken to Kate about them but wanted to grasp the reason for their strained relationship.

Now, Kate nibbled on cookies and spoke with her usual kindness to the girls who wandered by and stopped to talk.

After an appropriate amount of time, he nudged Kate's arm and whispered in her ear. "About ready?"

She nodded, a look of relief on her face, and he grinned, knowing she was probably hungry. "Tired of chips and dip, huh? And you want some 'real' food."

Though Kate grinned at Scott's comment, she felt nauseated. She'd struggled to maintain a sense of calm, then panicked, wondering if some ancient housemother might remember her face or recall her name. She'd been foolish. Most of the young staff wasn't much older than Kate's own daughter.

As they took leave, Kate waved goodbye, then stopped near a lone young lady. "Thanks for having us," Kate said to the quiet girl who reminded Kate of herself at that age.

"We're glad you came," she responded, her hand bracing the large swell of her belly.

Outside, Kate drew the refreshing, frigid air into her lungs. Unexpected, her frosty breath seemed warmer than the icy feelings that crept through her veins. Inside Madonna House, she'd forced herself to smile and make friendly conversation while her heart wanted to weep.

Kate assumed that nowadays facilities like Madonna House were uncommon. With the newer laws, most single, pregnant girls were allowed to attend their regular school and most kept their babies, but a few, tossed out by angry parents or hidden by well-meaning families much like her own, still found a haven at Madonna House.

"I hope that wasn't too unpleasant," Scott said, tucking her hand in his as they walked to the car.

"It was fine." She wished she could say something nicer, something more positive, but the words stuck in her throat.

Reaching the car, Scott pulled out the key and opened the door. His frozen breath hung on the air. "The whole world has changed, and it seems as if I haven't."

She heard it coming and slid into the car, hoping the darkness blocked the fear that rose to her face.

Scott closed the door, rounded the car, and climbed into the driver's seat. He turned the ignition key, then leaned over and kissed Kate's cheek. "I hope you don't mind spending time with an old-fashioned guy. I'm going to sound like your father, but I don't understand why kids get into these situations."

"They want to be popular," Kate murmured, peering through the passenger window, her face turned away from his, her mind tangled in the past.

"Popular? Really? I'd think they'd have more common sense."

"They don't," Kate said, fighting the tears that welled in her eyes. "They're desperate."

"I figure males think of promiscuity as a conquest—like St. George slaying the dragon or King Arthur seizing Excalibur. But females—"

"Want to be needed and loved. It boils down to that, Scott. Two little words and one big problem."

Scott grasped Kate's frigid hand and kissed her fingers. "And that's why I need you, Kate. You and I have the same convictions. Nothing could be better."

The winter moon slipped behind a cloud, and Kate's world turned as black as the night.

Chapter Fourteen

Scott added a log in the condo's fireplace. Glancing at Cass's computer now sitting in the niche of shelving, he chuckled to himself and couldn't wait to share his newest realization with Kate. Calling himself an old-fashioned guy was sadly appropriate. In a world of technology, why hadn't he or Kate thought about searching on a newspaper's Web site for information on the suspected apartment fire? After dinner, he planned to surprise her with surfing the Internet.

The aroma of tomatoes and spices drifted from the kitchen, and Scott returned to toss the salad. Though his culinary skills weren't exemplary, he could make a mean scampi, and he hoped steaming the rice wasn't beyond his talent. He'd never prepared dinner for Kate, though she had often surprised him with a home-cooked meal. Tonight, he'd promised her a taste of his gourmet skills.

In the dining alcove off the living room, Scott had hauled out Cass's fine china dinnerware—white ringed with a black-and-gold band. With black place mats and napkins, he added black-handled silverware. He'd even thought to pick up a small bouquet of flowers for the onyx vase with matching candlesticks he placed in the center of the table. He stood back, admiring the setting. He had outdone himself.

His mind filled with a mixture of thoughts and questions, Scott hoped this night would be special. His confession of love hadn't sat well with Kate, but he prayed that the idea had grown on her. At times, he was confident that Kate felt the same, that only her wavering self-worth kept them apart.

Other times, he feared that Kate's problem lay deeper, that he might never uncoil the knots of her uncertainty. He'd prayed for God to intervene—that the Lord would give him the strength and assurance that he and Kate were meant for each other. He felt it in his heart. But was it only...

The flash of car lights stretching across the wall alerted him, and Scott strode to the front window and glanced outside. Kate climbed from the car and hurried up the walk. When she stepped inside, she brought along the scent of brisk January air and sweet melons.

"Hi," he said, brushing a kiss on her cheek.

"Smells good," Kate said.

"So do you."

She grinned. "I meant whatever you're cooking."

Scott hung her coat in the closet, then took her

hand and guided her to the dining alcove. "Pretty fancy, huh?"

She nodded, but a look of apprehension rose in her face. "Almost like a special occasion," she said, searching his eyes.

"Only you. You're my special occasion." Though he smiled, a cold sinking sensation shivered through him. Was she fearing a proposal? Not tonight, but one day soon, he hoped to ask her to marry him. Would she respond with this same look of anxiety? He refused to worry about it tonight. He prayed God would direct him.

He sent her to the CD player to put on a disk, and Scott returned to the kitchen. Lifting the pot lid, he peeked at the rice, now fluffy and plump. Success! He pulled the salad from the refrigerator, dressed it, and carried it to the table. Then returned for the scampi and rice.

After the blessing, Scott handed the salad to Kate and dished up the entrée. With general chatter interspersed with compliments to the chef, they ate, but Scott's eyes were drawn to the computer, hoping that tonight Kate would get her answer.

After dinner, before Scott mentioned the child, Amber's name came into the conversation.

"I've been giving a lot of thought to Amber," Kate said. "I'm afraid Mrs. Yates isn't going to recover. Or if she does, she'll be unable to take care of Amber. You're the doctor. What do you think?"

"I agree. When I stopped by yesterday, the nurse told me she's had another stroke. Her status seems grave, and she's definitely comatose. No response at all.''

Kate leaned forward and ran her fingers through the length of her hair, then brushed the tresses behind her shoulder. "I'd like to be a foster parent to Amber. That's what I've been thinking. I want to take her home."

"Home? But Kate you work every day. How can you be a foster mother and spend your days at the Haven?"

"Mothers do it all the time, Scott. Having a child doesn't end a woman's career."

"But this is different. You'd be investigated. Scrutinized. Wouldn't they want to place a child in a home with two parents? Where the mother is home to be with the child?"

"Amber goes to school almost the same hours that I work. If I can offer her a good home, I don't think it should make a difference. You don't think I'd be a good parent?"

Scott shook his head. "Don't be silly. You'd make a wonderful mother. The best in the world...but it would be difficult."

"Life's difficult." A ragged sigh shuddered from her throat. "Anyway, once we can get to the library and find a way to locate Amber's parents, there'll be no need."

Remembering his plan, Scott's spirit lifted. "Speaking of that, I've had an interesting insight."

She snapped her head in his direction. "About what?"

"That I can bring the library to us."

A puzzled frown settled on her face. "What do you mean?"

Scott swung his hand toward the computer desk. "Technology, Kate. We're sitting here with a computer and a modem. We have access to the Internet and to the daily Detroit newspapers."

Kate's eyes widened and her frown vanished, replaced by an astonished grin. "I feel stupid. Why hadn't either of us thought of that before?"

"I'm not alone with that old-fashioned tag I mentioned. We were too caught up in the problem and didn't think."

Kate rose and took a step toward the computer. "So, can we?"

Scott rose to her side and wrapped his arms around her from behind, then scooted her along to the chair that faced the monitor. "Sit."

"No, you. I'm shaking so badly I can't even think."

Scott acquiesced and plopped into the desk chair. He hit the power button, and they waited silently as the computer booted up.

Kate's trembling hand rested on the chair arm, and Scott slid his palm over her icy fingers, praying the task was easy and productive.

When the desktop was ready, Scott clicked the mouse on the appropriate icons, listed his password, and typed the address into the key word slot. In another minute, the web site of a Detroit newspaper appeared.

"This is today's news," Kate said, the disappointment wilting her tone.

"Don't jump to conclusions," he said, scanning the choices. "I'm sure they have back issues." He moved the mouse and clicked Services, then Search.

"Archives," Kate yelled, poking the monitor where the word appeared.

In a heartbeat, Scott stared at another key word search. "Here goes." He typed in "Yates" and "fire," then filled in the date that the hospital had given. When he hit Search, Kate leaned over his back and gripped his shoulders. Finally, a headline appeared in the small box, Three Die in House Fire.

"Is that it?" she yelled, motioning to the sentence.

Scott scrolled down the incomplete article which ended abruptly. Red lettering followed the short blurb of information. "There's a $1.95 fee for the whole article," he said, reading the instructions. Using his credit card, he continued. Finally, the full article appeared.

The facts marched before him. Kate read in a whisper the reporter's words of the fire that destroyed an upper flat, killing Roland and Donna Yates, and their son James.

"Amber had a brother," Kate said, her voice hushed by the dire news. "Look." She pointed to the screen and read, "Also lost in the fire was the family's pet spaniel...Sparky."

Kate's ragged breath sounded behind him, then she whispered. "The day I handed Amber that toy puppy, she called it Sparky. She remembered the dog.''

Emotionally touched by the article, Scott scanned the report, detailing the event. ''Roland's mother and his youngest daughter Amber, who had spent the night with her grandmother in the lower flat, escaped with minor burns.''

Scott fell back against the chair. ''So it was a flat and not an apartment.''

Kate shrugged. ''Guess her drawing made us think apartment. Amber's father was an only child,'' she added, pointing to the final paragraph.

Scott scanned to the end and read the words himself.

''What about Donna Yates? There's no reference to her family.'' He twisted in the chair to face her.

Kate shrugged, her face filled with thought. In silence, she rested her crossed arms on the back of the desk chair and stared at the monitor.

Scott waited, knowing her mind was mulling through the information.

''I'm going to look into being a foster parent,'' Kate said. ''If something happens to Amber's grandmother, I'll be able to…'' Her voice halted and tears filled her eyes. ''I'd take her now, Scott. I really love that little girl, but I'm only setting myself up for hurt if Mrs. Yates pulls through…and I sure don't want to pray for anything else.''

''You can't let every kid at the Haven tear you up like this,'' Scott said, concern filling his thoughts.

''I don't. I never have before. There's just some-

thing about Amber. Something I can't explain."
Disappointed at his attitude, she bit the corner of her
lip, wishing he'd encourage her decision instead of
listing all the problems. She searched his face for a
flicker of understanding.

He closed the programs and rose from the chair,
then captured her in his arms. "Okay, but I worry
about you."

"It's a lot of things, Scott. It's not just for Amber
or me. Jesus said, 'Whoever welcomes one of these
little children welcomes me.' It's the Lord's will,
too."

"I know, Kate."

Nestled beside him, Kate wished she could explain the truth, how Amber would fill her desire to
be a mother and would release the guilt and love
she'd bound inside her.

"Amber's special," Kate said. "And if I
never..." She faltered. How could she say that if
she never married, Amber could make amends for
her adopted baby daughter? She could atone for her
sin.

Scott eyed her. "Never what?"

"Well, if I never...try to be a foster parent, I'll
never know." The cover-up tumbled out of her
mouth.

"It's a big step. I don't know." He circled his
hand gently across her shoulder blades. "Kate, have
you thought about how your parents will react to
this?"

She stiffened in his arms. Her parents? What did he mean?

"Please, don't get upset," he said, apparently sensing her tension. He guided her toward the sofa and sat down beside her.

"It doesn't really matter," Kate said. "You saw them in action. They have their opinions and not much will change them. My parents' interpretation of God's will is different from many people's."

"I saw that when we were together." He slid his arm around her shoulder. "Kate, I know why they're angry at Kristin. Christian parents don't accept divorce, especially their own child's, but why are they so uptight with you?"

She froze, unable to think. Unable to speak.

"I'm sorry. I shouldn't have asked. But whatever it was, Kate, you were probably just a kid. You made some kind of mistake." He eyed her. "You got in trouble with the law or...?" He paused as if waiting for her to fill in the blank. "It couldn't have been that bad."

Kate felt him tense.

He stepped back and peered into her face. Fear altered his compassionate face. "You aren't divorced, too, are you?" His face had paled.

"No," she said, finding her voice, "I was never married." But she should have been for all she'd done. The truth propelled through her like buckshot. "It was long ago. It's over."

"But it's not. You've suffered for some kind of infraction...for too long, I think. If this is why you're afraid to love me, Kate, please stop fighting it. Just love me.''

"I can't love you, Scott. I can't love anyone. I'll never marry. Now, I've said it, and as soon as you understand, the better it will be for us both. I'm not worth the anguish. You deserve someone—''

She stopped not knowing what else to say. The expression on his face twisted her heart and sent an ache coursing through her body.

"You can toss me aside, Kate, but I'm not giving up on you.''

She stared across the room at the computer monitor that had sent her hopes flying, and now she was spiraling downward in a fatal nosedive. Amber had been only one dream. Scott, the other. Together, they made her world whole. Could she trust Scott? Could she tell him that she wasn't the virgin he prized? That she was used goods. Not a rape. Not an accident. But a planned activity, tossing away all that was important in hopes that she would be popular like Kristin.

"Kate?''

Scott's sad voice touched her ear, and she lifted her head. "I'm okay. Give me time, Scott.''

"You can have all the time you need, Kate. But please don't push me away. I have my own guilt...my own hurt.''

Kate studied his face, wanting to ask him what he meant. But if she couldn't talk to him, how could she ask him to bear his heart? She needed to pray for God's help…for the Lord's will. If Scott loved her enough to put up with her constant turmoil, she needed to ask God for guidance. Yet, she feared that Scott deserved more than she could give.

Chapter Fifteen

When Kate opened the door just before dinner, the flower deliveryman surprised her. He held a lovely floral arrangement of white lilies, delicate pink tulips, and rose-hued carnations. She carried the flowers into the house and noted the gift card. Scott's message peeked out of the blossoms. "With the Lord, all things are possible."

Admiring the lovely flowers, Kate felt a tender longing flow through her. She plucked the card from the bouquet and ran her finger along Scott's familiar script—the long slash across the double *t*, the snake-curved *s*.

Always thoughtful, Scott had been gentle and persistent since their dinner at Cass's. That evening the moment the conversation reached its peak, Kate had expected to tell him goodbye, but the words bunched in her throat, and "I love you" filled her mind instead. And she truly did.

But the foreboding remained.

Many nights, she tossed and turned in her bed, trying to create a dialogue—a way to explain herself, a way to break the news of her unchaste youth, a way to ask forgiveness before she spit out the horrible words.

Pretending she was Scott, Kate mentally recited and listened to her tale, then cringed when the words smacked her across the face—a story she already knew. The test run failed. How could she second-guess Scott's reaction? Yes, he loved her. He'd told her often, though she'd only uttered "I love you" once, afraid that saying it would make a commitment she couldn't handle.

Two years younger, handsome and chaste, Scott had much to offer a pure Christian woman. Sure, Kate was a Christian, but pure...? And no matter what she did, she could never bring back the chastity that she longed to give her husband.

Why hadn't she realized the truth of that terrible moment when she willingly slid down against the seat cushion in the back of Ron's car and watched the rain running in rivulets like the tears that rolled down her cheeks? Her knotted hands dug into her palms as his square, muscled frame arched above her, then the undefinable moment—the loss of her morals, her faith, her innocence. Why hadn't she realized that the deep piercing hurt would stab her heart and leave her feeling sorrowful and unworthy for the rest of her life?

Corralling her anguish, Kate pulled her thoughts

back to the lovely bouquet. In the last dredges of winter, Scott had sent her a little taste of spring. The thought caught in her mind. Scott's love offered her the same, the promise of rebirth following the bitter years of dying. She buried her nose in the flowers and drew in the sweet, promising scent.

"How do you rate?"

Kate turned toward Phyllis's voice. "I didn't hear you come in."

"That's because I'm crawling." Phyllis grinned and crumbled into a chair. "Planning a wedding is too much work. I tried to convince Darren we should run away. Elope and send a telegram."

"You'd never do that," Kate said, shaking her head at her friend's foolish idea.

"I know, but it sounds good." She gestured toward the arrangement. "So, who sent the flowers?"

"Take a guess."

"Oh, him," Phyllis said, feigning surprise. "When are the two of you going to make the big announcement?"

Empty hope plodded through Kate's veins. "I don't know, Phyl. Maybe never."

"You're kidding. Why?"

"I'm too old to settle down. I'm set in—"

"Poor excuse, Kate. You've been sputtering around here for the past weeks filling out paperwork to become a foster parent. You don't think that will change your life and make you settle down?"

Kate shrugged, hoping to mute the sadness that

sat like a rock against her heart. "I'm too old to manage that many changes."

"Don't hand me that." Phyllis leaned forward, peering into Kate's face. "Don't you love Scott, Kate?" Her expression announced her disbelief. "I can't imagine that you don't. I know he loves you."

Kate skirted the issue, relating her upbringing again, her inability to love, her fear of commitment.

Phyllis listened quietly for a few minutes, then pressed her palm against the air like a traffic cop. "Stop, Kate. You're making excuses. What you say and do is contradictory. Upbringing, sure, that can be a problem, but I've seen you with Amber and Scott. You have love spilling out of you, and with foster care, you're promising a commitment to Amber. So why can't you do the same for Scott?"

Kate tried to respond, but Phyllis rose and shook her head. "Look, if you don't love Scott enough to marry him, that's one thing. But if you're handing me excuses for some other reason, please don't. You owe me nothing, Kate. I owe you."

"You don't owe me a thing. What do you mean?"

"I've lived here in your home, I've taken advantage of your friendship, I've burdened you with my ups and downs. You've put up with my idiosyncrasies, my antics—"

"Now, you stop," Kate said, rising and putting her arms around Phyllis. "I love Scott. I love him with all my heart." She lifted her teary eyes to Phyllis's tense, confused face. "I have some personal problems to resolve. I can't do anything until I deal with those issues. That's the long and short of it.''

"Can I help?'' Phyllis asked, moisture pooling on her lashes.

"No. I have to do it alone.''

"But—''

Kate pressed her forehead against Phyllis's. "Don't ask, Phyl. I'll tell you when it's time. Please understand?''

She felt her friend's head nod against her own. When she calmed, she stepped back and forced a smile to her tearstained face. "Now, tell me about the wedding plans. I can't wait.''

Looking over her shoulder, Kate chuckled at Scott, paint-splattered from head to toe. "Did I ever mention you look good in pink?''

His mouth drooped, and he peered at his spotted jeans and T-shirt. "Did I ever mention I'm not a painter?''

Seeing his silly expression, Kate sputtered a laugh. "I'll agree you're no Rembrandt. But I hope you can wallpaper.''

He shook his head and bent down to add paint to the roller.

Kate returned to her task and picked up the paint-brush. She loved the shade she'd chosen for the up-stairs bedroom—as delicate as a cherry blossom. Amber would love it...if things went as planned.

Kate sighed. Her application for the foster parent license had been accepted, her finances verified, her mental and physical health scrutinized. She'd provided three character references. They'd even checked her for a criminal record. So far, she'd passed all the requirements. Now, she expected a home visit in the next couple weeks. Having the room ready was at the top of her list.

Amber. With wavering emotion, Kate struggled, facing the paradoxical reality. If Mrs. Yates improved, Amber would returned to live with her grandmother. Kate would be joyful for Amber, her own sorrow salved by the child's reunion. Until she faced that day, the room would be a little girl's dream: ribbons, lace and ruffles.

Scott had even let her drag him to the Birmingham Decorating Shop and waited while she poured through books of wallpaper samples. Cartoons, clowns, ballerinas, fairy tales, pandas—nothing seemed to fit until she noticed a dainty print paper, posies tied with lengths of pink ribbon on a white background, as delicate and ethereal as Amber.

Kate peeked at Scott, busy behind her, and grinned. He put down the roller, blew a stream of air from his lungs, and perched on top of the four-rung wooden ladder. "I hope all this work isn't going to waste."

"I'm thinking positive. So far, they've approved my application. The agency only has a few more things to check."

"Look at it this way, if something goes wrong, you've decorated your guest room."

Kate gaped at the pastel walls. "Pink? I hope dear old Uncle Albert doesn't come for a visit."

Laughing, Scott rose from the stool and walked to her side, nuzzling his head against hers, but keeping his smeared hands out of reach. "Things'll be fine, I'm sure."

With a peck on the cheek, he turned back to the wall and his roller. Kate dipped the brush into the paint can, adding a glossy coat to the moldings and windowsills.

The room hummed with their efforts, and when Kate finished the trim, she stepped back and admired the effect. She checked Scott's progress. With even strokes, Scott rolled the second coat of color on the final wall. Tomorrow, all she had left was the wallpaper. An easy job, she hoped—one single, unbroken wall.

Admiring the dainty colored walls, she faced her fears. No matter how she tried to convince herself, she'd feel devastated if, for some reason, Amber were placed in another foster home.

"Done," Scott said, stepping back and dropping the roller onto the pan. "Looks good, if I do say so."

"It does. And the wallpaper will make it even better."

"I'm on staff that day," he said, halting her inquiry. He chuckled at his wily excuse. "Listen, I'll clean up this mess If you'll order a pizza...or two. I'm starving."

His offer sounded like a good deal, and she scurried off to clean up and make the call.

Scott lugged the paint and supplies to the basement and stood over the laundry tub, scouring the brushes and roller.

Worried about Kate, he imagined her disappointment if things didn't go as she had planned. Foster parenting wasn't easy, especially for someone unmarried and holding down a full-time job. Like an arrow, the word *unmarried* pierced his emotions. If Scott had anything to say, Kate would be married in a minute.

Grasping the fingernail brush, he attacked his paint-spattered hands. Even when he first met Kate, he recalled his hesitation to get romantically involved. Though he found her interesting and attractive, he wanted no part of the ups and downs of romance. He'd lost faith in women and himself. And he'd felt shame for his religious convictions.

That was the brunt of his problem with Lana. She'd made him ashamed to be a Christian—embarrassed to stand up for his moral values, his belief that chastity wasn't only important, but was God's directive.

In the past months as he'd drawn closer to Kate, he'd let those old fears slide into his locked trunk of unwanted memories. Now he was falling all over himself, trying to convince Kate to love him. Maybe, the real issue was to trust him. But how could she?

Kate knew he had old hurts and regrets. He'd

hinted at them enough times. Could that be what she was waiting for? Would she think that if he trusted her enough to open his old wounds, then she'd be willing to reveal hers?

Though a sense of relief marched through him, anxiety rattled the key to the truth deep in his mind. Maybe he'd talk today. But he'd wait for the right moment. Definitely not before the pizza.

Spreading the brushes and roller out to dry, Scott soaped, rinsed his hands and arms, dried them, then checked his face in the lavatory mirror. He scraped off a few telltale splatters and rinsed. Pulling a comb from his back pocket, he dragged it through his hair and deemed himself ready.

As he climbed the basement stairs, he heard Kate in the kitchen. When he stepped into the room, he saw she had set the table with paper plates and salad bowls.

Kate smiled over her shoulder. Her face gleamed from the scrubbing, and he imagined what she might look like in the morning, fresh from a shower.

At the counter, she was tossing salad greens into a bowl. "Giorgio's doesn't have salads so I thought I'd make one."

"Great," he said, slipping behind her and snatching a piece of cucumber from the greens.

"How do you expect me to do this with you hanging on me?"

"I don't," he said, sweeping her around into his arms.

He popped a kiss on her nose, then grinned when

he spotted the paring knife clutched in her hand. He cautiously pivoted her back to the counter with her laughter ringing in his ears.

Along with her laugh, the doorbell jingled, and Scott hurried off to answer, hoping it was the pizza delivery. With his wish fulfilled, he hoisted the two containers over his head, chuckling that she'd taken him literally. In the kitchen, they settled down to tall glasses of soda, the garden salad and the thick, hot squares of deep-dish pizza.

When he pushed back from the table, Kate arched an eyebrow and jiggled the cardboard box containing the eight slices. "I thought you said order two."

"I didn't mean large." Though he gave her a wink, his earlier thoughts sat on his mind, and he wished he could chow down a couple more pieces to delay the inevitable.

He rose and helped Kate clear the table, then wandered back into the living room, tempted to snap on the TV or do anything to avoid the nettled thoughts that prodded him.

In a moment, Kate joined him, carrying their refreshed tumblers of ice and soda. He grasped his and slid it on the nearby table. Kate chose an adjacent chair and sat. "I hope that paint smell doesn't hang around too long."

"It won't," he said, wishing the same for the words that lodged in his throat. He pulled his T-shirt away from his Adam's apple and swallowed.

"Kate, you know how I feel about you, and

please, don't stop me. I have some things I really
want to get off my back."

"What things?" Her face tensed, and she knotted
her arms against her chest. "Did I do something?"

"No, nothing like that."

Her face relaxed.

If he were honest, he'd tell her she *had* done
something—not love him in return. But in his heart,
he believed Kate did love him. She just didn't know
it, yet.

"This is about me, Kate."

He sensed he'd piqued her interest. She rested her
elbow on the chair arm nearest him and balanced
her chin in her hand. "What is it?"

"I told you a long time ago that I had something
that bothered me. Things I'd done that made me
ashamed."

"Please, Scott, no, it's not necessary—"

"It is Kate. I want to be completely honest with
you, and it's not so much what I did, but how I
reacted. That's the part that bothers me most."

She didn't respond, but she didn't try to stop him,
either. He continued. "I've always been a bookworm of sorts. I suppose part of me has tried to pay
my folks back for loving me. Just a quirk of being
an adopted kid, I guess. They never gave me cause
to question their love. But somewhere in me I felt
different from others, not as loveable maybe."

He grasped the strands of his rambling concepts
and quickly tried to tie them together. "Getting to
the point, when I was in college, I met an attractive

girl. Lana. She was wilder than me. More adventurous. She'd smoke sometimes and have a drink. I knew I shouldn't get involved with her, but she was enticing…and to be honest, one of the first girls that captured my interest.''

As if puzzled, Kate shifted in the seat, sipped her soda, and leaned against the cushion, her face intent. He could almost see her counseling wheels turning.

''Anyway, besides the other things Lana tried, she was eager to learn about passion. Sometimes when kids leave home, they want to try all the things that their parents forbid. I have to admit I was tempted. Lana made herself available, but I avoided getting involved. The more I made excuses the more she chided and manipulated. Finally, I got up the nerve to admit I believed in chastity.''

Kate's face paled and a look of concern washed over her. Scott pushed himself forward, wanting to finish his confession.

''She laughed, Kate. 'You're a virgin,' she said, as if I were some kind of freak. I groveled in self-pity. She tempted me, pushed me as far as I let her, and then she told me to take her home.''

His voice caught, and shame filled him again, recalling that day. ''I should've stood up for myself and my faith, Kate. I let her attitude make me embarrassed that I believed in God's Word. I should've told her to leave, instead of letting her make me the fool.''

Kate leaned forward. ''But the sin was hers, not yours, Scott. You stood your ground. You didn't let her push you to do something you thought was wrong. You were better than she was."

Her defense touched him, and he wished she'd do the same, tell him her past pain so he could stand up for her.

"I'm not telling you for your social work skills, Kate. I just wanted you to know that we all have things that we hate remembering, shameful memories that hang on in the back of our minds like leeches."

Kate straightened herself in the chair. "I didn't mean to sound like a social worker. I'm sure that was an awful time for you, Scott. You're a great guy and it's obvious you didn't let it destroy you or weaken your faith. Maybe it strengthened you. Made you more sure of your beliefs."

It felt easy to tell her now, and he decided to add the last chapter of the story, hoping she would see the depth of his scar and encourage her to talk with him.

"She tried to humiliate me a few months later," he said. "On my way to class, she stopped me. She was latched on to some big strapping dude that she left standing alone while she strode across the grass.

"She had an arrogant smile plastered on her face and a stack of books propped on her belly. It took only a minute for me to realize she was pregnant. She told me she was getting married. As she left, she hollered over her shoulder that it was a shame I wasn't a real man."

Kate released a gasp. "You are a real man," Kate

said. "More than that, you're perfect. You listen to God and do what He asks. That's why you deserve the best."

Scott faltered hearing her voice. He sensed that a distance had stretched between them, as if a drawbridge had lifted and a moat separated them. And he didn't know why.

Chapter Sixteen

Kate shifted the paperwork on her office desk, unable to concentrate. She couldn't get Scott's confession out of her mind. Like a social worker, she'd listened with concern, analyzing the situation and helping him face the truth. Then like a snake slithering out of the tall grass, his words chilled her to the bone.

As if a wedge had been hammered between them, Kate faced her own truth. No matter how much she loved him, a relationship was impossible. Even if Scott said he had forgiven her sinful behavior, she'd know he never could. He stood up for himself against Lana, despite how he felt. Rather than making a sexual conquest—using her willingness for a new experience—he lived by his faith, like David against Goliath. But Kate had embraced sin and, like Bathsheba, had hurt her family and lost her child.

A tap on the door roused her from the dark thoughts, and she looked toward the door.

Phyllis stepped into the office. "Got a minute?"

"Sure."

"I just want to remind you we're shopping after work for bridesmaid dresses."

"How could I forget? You all but tattooed it on my forehead."

Laughing, Phyllis caved onto a chair. "I'm a little preoccupied I guess. I've been meaning to ask you about Amber. I saw her in the hallway earlier. How's she doing?"

"Good. I think we're making some strides. Besides remembering Sparky, she now remembers the fire...vaguely, mainly how her grandmother carried her outside."

"I'd say that's good progress. How about the bad dreams?"

"Better. She has them once in a while, but they don't affect her like they did. That's the best thing that's happened."

Phyllis yawned and rubbed her eyes. "How about her parents? Any memories?"

Kate shook her head. "Nothing really, and I don't want to push. Anyway, I wonder if she spent most of her time with her grandma."

Phyllis shrugged. "Maybe her parents both worked. Speaking of which," she said, standing up, "I'd better get back. I'm so lazy today." She headed toward the door, then stopped. "Think about colors."

"Colors?" Kate asked.

"For the gowns."

Kate laughed. "Do you think of anything else?"

"Not until May 26. Two and half months."

"I can't wait," Kate said, realizing how much time went into planning even a small wedding.

Phyllis hurried from the room, and Kate flipped open a file, staring at the page. How would she feel if this were her wedding? A flutter of jealousy shivered into her thoughts and out again.

She glanced through the window, seeing the tiny nubs of green poking from the trees. In spring a young man's fancy turns to thoughts of love. The old saying jogged through her head, and she gave it a twist. Not only man's, but woman's. She blamed it on Noah…and God, animals marching two by two.

Her telephone rang, sending Noah and his animals running for cover. She snatched up the receiver and said hello. When she heard Scott's voice, a ripple of longing waved through her. "What's up?" she asked.

"My procrastination got the best of me today."

She lifted her eyebrows. Always, she had to sort through his puzzling words. "What's that mean?"

"It means I called Pastor Ray to check on Mrs. Finkell."

"Ah, guilt with a capital *G*. I thought she was in a nursing home."

"That was only for a short time while she recuperated and learned to give herself insulin shots."

"So, she's back home?" Kate asked.

"Uh-huh, I thought we could go and visit her after work. What do you say?"

"I say I'm going to the bridal shop to look at bridesmaid gowns with Phyllis."

"Oh."

She heard the disappointment in his voice. "Sorry. Do you want to postpone?"

"No, I called her. She's expecting me."

"Well, have fun and give her my best." Kate said, picturing poor Scott trying to conjure up conversation to interest the elderly woman.

"Will I see you later?" he asked.

"Sounds good," Kate said.

A lengthy pause dragged through the line. "Could you do me a favor?"

She hesitated, curious as to what he had in mind. "Sure, what?"

"Check out those wedding dresses while you're there, okay?"

After she hung up, she sat frozen in place. Though she knew she'd responded with a witty comment, she had no recollection of what she said.

Pulling dollar bills from his pocket, Scott paid for the small spray of carnations and fern. He wished he had stock in a florist shop for all the flowers he'd purchased lately. He'd been persistent, doing everything to show Kate how much he loved her.

But this bouquet wasn't for Kate. They were for Mrs. Finkell. He was disappointed that Kate couldn't come along. Besides enjoying her company, he'd thought she'd take him off the hook of finding things to talk about. But he'd come up with something.

He knew he'd erred when he teased Kate about checking out the wedding dresses. A deafening silence had filled the line before she sputtered back a short response. He should have thought before opening his mouth.

His sister's wedding was approaching with the speed of a comet, and with that thought, a wave of frustration washed over him. He'd hoped to be engaged to Kate by Phyllis's wedding date, but Kate's acceptance was as slow as a child waiting for Christmas. He wasn't sure his efforts had made a second's worth of headway.

Outside, he headed for his car, and after placing the flowers on the passenger seat, he pulled into traffic and headed toward Mrs. Finkell's home.

Scott parked in the driveway of the familiar house, and the door opened before he reached the porch steps. The older woman eyed the bouquet with a growing smile.

"For me?" she asked, her arm extended toward the flowers.

"None other." Scott handed her the carnations and stepped inside.

"Thank you," she said, burying her nose in the bouquet. "No one brings me flowers anymore. My daughter sends an arrangement on Mother's Day, sometimes."

Scott followed her into the tiny kitchen where she pulled a vase from under the sink and filled it with water.

"Need some help?" Scott asked, watching her shaking fingers try to undo the florist's packaging.

She stepped aside, and Scott went to work. "You look better than the last time I saw you," he said, removing the wrapping.

"I'm much better, thanks to you. I've thought of you so often, wanting to tell you how grateful I am. I could be dead, you know." She lifted her wrinkled face to his and grinned.

"I know," he said, "but you're fit as a fiddle, as they say."

"Sure am." She plopped the flowers into the vase and tucked the ferns around the blossoms. "There now. Real pretty." She turned from the sink. "So, could I get you a drink?"

"No, I'm fine."

She nodded, grasped the flowers, and headed back to the living room, her voice sailing over her shoulder as Scott followed. "You're fine, huh? I've been wondering about that young lady and you."

She set the vase on a table and motioned toward an easy chair. "Have a seat."

"Kate, you mean?" Scott asked, sinking into the cushion.

Mrs. Finkell settled on the sofa. "I think that's her name. Pretty girl with blond hair and a smile as bright as sunshine."

"That's her," Scott said as Kate's image rose in his mind.

"So, you two getting married?"

"I wish."

"What's that mean? Did you ask her?"

"Not exactly, but—"

The woman tossed her head backward with a chuckle. "Do you need an old lady to tell you how to court a girl? They never say they'll marry you unless you ask."

Her words tickled him, but she'd hit upon the truth. He'd thought his intention was clear. But maybe not. Or was Kate waiting for something else? Had he missed a clue? Had he done something wrong to discourage her? "She knows how I feel, but Kate says she needs time. I'm thinking she—"

"Time, you say?"

He nodded.

"I suppose women say that. Might've myself. But time means there's hope."

Her puzzling words were lost to him. "What?"

"If she didn't care, she'd say so. A woman knows when it's no. It's the yes that's harder to say."

Looking at her creased face and white hair, Scott wondered if she meant Victorian women or today's.

"You think I'm too old to know what I'm talking about?"

Scott laughed out loud, positive she was a mind reader. "I'm thinking that might not hold true for modern women."

"Women are women. It's not playing hard to get.

It's wanting to know their hearts.'' She pressed her gnarled fingers against her chest. ''Everything happens right here,'' she said, tapping two fingers against her cotton print dress. ''Lifetime commitments don't come easy.''

''You're right about that.'' Scott thought of his own struggles, and how he'd finally faced them.

''Now, the big question. Do you *really* court her?''

''You mean send flowers and say 'I love you'?''

''That, too, but I mean let your actions do the work. I've seen many a bouquet and endearments that held empty promises. Actions count.''

Actions count. The thought rumbled through his mind. He'd asked himself what he'd done wrong. Maybe the question was what hadn't he done. Amber came to mind. He'd definitely discouraged Kate's idea of being a foster parent...except for helping her paint. His words weren't encouraging. But he was protecting Kate, that was all. Then, another ''hadn't done'' came to him. He hadn't trusted that, in time, she'd tell him what pressed so heavily on her heart.

''I hit a sore spot, I see,'' Mrs. Finkell said.

''You've given me things to think about. I can tell you all the things I've done to let Kate know how much I care, but you've made me think of things I *haven't* done.''

Mrs. Finkell nodded, her pale eyes misting. ''Love is give and take. But it's lots more give. That's a hard lesson to learn. I remember when I was a young bride, I tried being thoughtful, but I did it for the wrong reason.''

"What's the wrong reason?" Scott asked, amazed that this white-haired lady had become a biblical Mrs. King Solomon.

"The wrong reason is wanting something back. Never give to get. Give because you love the lady so much that if she gave you nothing back, you wouldn't give a hoot.''

Her words spiraled through him, and he grabbed at the dangling strings of thought, trying to weave them together into a solid understanding. First thing he needed was prayer. The Bible taught to give and you'd be rewarded, but the Bible didn't say give *so* you are rewarded. There's a difference. Mrs. Finkell put her finger on it.

As soon as Scott entered the house, tears rushed down Kate's cheeks.

"What's wrong?" Scott blurted, rushing to her side and taking her in his arms.

"Mrs. Yates died this morning, and I had to tell—''

"Amber," he finished, as her sobs overtook her. She buried her face against his chest.

He held her in his arms, letting the tension wash away. When Kate lifted her face, her puffy eyes were rimmed with moisture and damp rivulets clung to her cheeks.

"I'm sorry," she said. "I don't mean to be so emotional. Telling Amber was unbelievably difficult, and then, I know the Haven has to arrange placement for her…and my approval hasn't been finalized yet. I don't know what to do.''

Without responding, Scott guided her to the sofa and sat beside her, resting her head on his shoulder.

''I'd think the Haven could be reasonable, Kate. They know you and they know Amber. Why can't they—''

''State regulations, Scott. If it were up to my director, she'd let me bring her home.'' She raised her head. ''I've been thinking…and I—I want to adopt Amber.''

''Adopt her? But—'' He stopped, remembering his talk with Mrs. Finkell two weeks earlier about giving without expecting anything in return.

Kate continued, ''I know you don't like the idea. You don't even like—''

''That's not true, Kate. Amber's a wonderful kid who deserves a loving parent. You're the most loving woman I know. It's a perfect match. She even looks a little like you. It's *you* I've worried about. You being hurt or disappointed if Amber was returned to her grandmother.''

''I worried about it, too, but now…things are different.''

''They sure are.'' Still, a new thought poked his fading concerns. ''Will they look for more family now?''

She drew the back of her hand across her misty eyes. ''Yes, but I think they'll learn what we already know. Even if they find someone, I doubt they'll take her, especially if they know someone wants to adopt.''

Conviction planted itself firmly in Scott's mind. He loved Kate, and he wanted to marry her no matter what. And today was as good as any to tell her.

''Why sit in here?'' he asked, grappling for a few more minutes to organize his words. ''Let's go outside. What do you say?''

Kate nodded, grabbing a sweater from the closet, but when they stepped off the back porch, she faltered, raising her hands into the air. ''It's like spring.''

''Told you,'' he said, slipping his arm around her shoulders and heading for the glider. ''Look at the flowers popping up. Remember when we first met? We sat out here, and all I could smell was lilacs...and you.''

She nudged him. ''Liar.''

''You're sweeter than any lilac, Kate.''

She grasped the arm of the glider and sat, ignoring his comment. ''I like spring,'' she said. ''Everything's new and fresh. Wish we could do that to our minds.''

''You can. Gardens don't grow without effort. It just takes work. If you let the weeds take over, they kill the flowers. Cleaning out the mind's the same thing.'' He lifted his arm and rested it across the seat back.''

''I've been praying a lot,'' Kate said. ''Praying that I can give things to God and not hang on to them. I guess I like weeds. Those problems sprout in my mind and cover all the good things.''

''That's what I mean.'' His heart galloped, wondering if today was the day she'd finally open up.

Kate straightened and faced him. ''Oh, well, enough of that. Let's talk about something more pleasant.''

The gallop halted, and his heart mired in disappointment. Still, Scott refused to stop now. He had something more pleasant to suggest—much more pleasant.

He swiveled on the seat and captured her chin in his hand. His chest swelled with the surprise in Kate's eyes, and he lowered his lips, enjoying the gentle feel of her mouth against his. She did love him. He was positive.

When he drew back, her eyes searched his.

''What brought that on?'' she asked.

''Do I need a reason to kiss you, other than the obvious?''

She lowered her head. ''I'm scared, Scott. My life is about to change and I'm praying I'm making the right decision—that what I'm doing for Amber isn't motivated by my own agenda.''

''What agenda?'' Her comment left him puzzled.

''You know what I mean. Doing it for the wrong reason.''

Wrong reason. Mrs. Finkell's words shot through him like an arrow. Often he'd done things for the wrong reason, but today was different. He drew in a deep breath, garnering the courage he'd need to see him through.

"And that leads me to another idea," Scott said, sending up a silent, speedy prayer. "Since you're in the change mode, I have an additional one for you."

Her head jerked toward him, a look of bewilderment and dread inching across her face. "What?"

"Marry me, Kate. I've wanted this for a long time, and—"

"Oh Scott, this isn't a good time to—"

"It's never been a good time. But for once, I'm doing something without expecting anything in return, Kate. You love Amber, and having a husband will make adoption easier. It might even speed up the foster parent decision, who knows?"

She opened her mouth to speak, but Scott pressed his index finger on her lips to stifle her words. "Don't talk. Let me finish. I know you have fears and problems. I expect nothing from you, Kate. Be my wife, and we can pray that God makes things right for us. There are no strings. I mean this from my heart."

He pulled his finger away from her lips, watching tears well in her eyes, and like a dam that collapsed, a torrent of emotions spilled over her like a waterfall.

"Kate, please, don't cry. I didn't want you to cry."

"It's not you, Scott. It's me," she said, her words mingled with her sobs.

"But I love you the way you are. All the surprises, the laughs, the tears, everything. I want you, Kate.''

''I've dreamed of this day,'' she whispered. ''In the back of my mind, I pictured this moment...but I never completed the dream. I never sensed how I'd answer.'' She brushed the tears from her hands knotted in her lap. ''I need to think. I need to pray, Scott.'' She lifted her eyes. ''Can you give me a little time?''

Mrs. Finkell's shaky voice sailed into Scott's mind. *But time means there's hope.* ''You can have all the time you need, Kate.'' He repeated the phrase over and over in his head. Time means hope.

Chapter Seventeen

Peering through the window into the backyard, Kate felt her heart lift as she watched Amber playing with a neighborhood child. Somewhere in her moments of panic, she stopped and prayed, prayed from the depths of her heart, and God had heard the prayer. Letting God handle problems was the wisest decision, yet the hardest task a person had to face.

Kate remembered how often she'd wrestled with her fears, pinning them to the floor, only to have them rise again and capture her in a stronghold for the count of ten. Why hadn't she learned that God moved mountains, yet carried the lambs in his bosom. For so long, she'd needed mountains moved and God's shepherding. Kate still needed the Lord.

With Scott's proposal pinioned in her thoughts, Kate's eyes filled with tears. His compassion and kindness, with the offer of marriage, touched her heart, but she didn't want his pity or self-sacrifice to make her dream come true. He was the best man she knew—the best she would ever know.

Now, God had blessed her with Amber, and the adoption papers were filed. Scott hadn't mentioned his kind offer again, but continued being part of her life—and Amber's.

Each day the proposal rattled in her conscience, pushing her to give him a kind and tender refusal. Avoidance didn't sit well with Kate.

Her reluctance was Phyllis's wedding. She and Scott were part of the bridal party. If tension happened between them, their attitudes could set the wedding on edge. She'd wait until after.

Kate turned away from the window and filled a glass with tap water. She took a long drink, analyzing her thoughts. If she were honest, her hesitation had to do with more than the wedding.

She'd talked to God and read her Bible, seeking a way to make her sinful confession. She owed that to Scott. Why? Because she loved him. But he deserved more than she could give. She was used goods, damaged merchandise. Scott merited the purest of all that was good.

Setting the glass on the counter, Kate floundered for a sense of serenity. If not a husband, God had given her a child—a child to nurture and to love, a chance to redeem herself. She'd opened her arms to Amber, just as God had opened His loving arms to her.

Kate flung open the back door and wandered outside. The new play set had been installed in the back of the yard, and she headed toward the glider, breathing in the sweet lilac-filled air. Amber's and her friend's giggles rose on the warm breeze, and the sun kissed Kate's arms, helping her feel nearly whole again. Nearly.

She sat on the glider, stretching her legs in front of her. Happiness shuffled along her spine, hearing Amber's content voice. When she lowered her head for a moment, her focus shifted to an army of ants, marching up the hill and another trooping down. Kate recalled a similar incident a year earlier. Gooseflesh rose on her arms. So much had happened since then.

As if it were yesterday, she remembered that special afternoon when she announced to no one in particular that she needed to take hold of her life. And moments later, she was wielding a flowered umbrella in Scott's face. The memory tugged a hearty chuckle from her chest.

"What's so funny?"

Kate lurched upward.

Scott stood a few feet away, his arms burdened with the largest stuffed bear Kate had ever seen.

"Scott," Amber yelled from the jungle gym and rushed to his side.

"Here you are, sunshine," he said, plopping the bear into her outstretched arms.

"That thing is as big as she is," Kate called, smiling at the mammoth stuffed animal.

Amber clutched the bear against her chest and waddled to Kate's side. "Look at my present."

"I can't miss it, sweetie. It's almost bigger than you are."

"But I love it," Amber said, plopping the toy on the glider beside Kate, then running with a leap into Scott's arms.

He wrapped her in a giant hug, and Amber pecked his cheek.

"Thank you," she said, her voice piping with excitement.

Amber's friend, Carrie, joined them, and the poor bear was dragged across the grass by the two girls, chattering about taking the toy down the slide and on the swing.

Scott grinned and dropped beside Kate. "You're almost as cute as Amber, Katie," he said, lifting her hand and kissing her fingers.

"You shouldn't have bought her that bear. It cost a fortune," Kate said.

"She's worth it. All the women I love are worth more than rubies."

"You sound biblical."

He gave her a wink. "That...and more."

The past months during their time together, Kate had finally learned to decode many of Scott's vague comments. She knew what he meant. The "more" he referred to was his love for her. The idea rattled her. Not wanting to deal with it, she shifted gears.

"Did you pick up the tux?"

"Sure did. Are you getting nervous?"

"Me?" Kate asked. "Tonight's only the rehearsal."

"I know, but I'm nervous. Best man has to re-member, well, the ring and——"

"And the ring," she said with a chuckled. "I have to lift her veil, hold the bouquet and crawl around on the floor a million times to straighten Phyllis's gown. They should retitle the job Cham-bermaid of Honor."

"Very original," Scott said, sliding his arm around her and nestling her to his side.

"You smell sweet," he said.

"It's the lilacs," she said. "You seem to get us confused."

He laughed.

Kate rested her head against his shoulder, watch-ing the children and the giant bear, but thinking about Scott. She didn't question whether Scott cared about her, but she wondered if he'd mentally re-scinded his proposal since Amber arrived.

Whether he had or not, Kate had to give him an answer. Marrying Scott would be a dream, a won-derful dream. But she couldn't marry without laying her life out in front of him. Marriage was based on honesty. But she wasn't sure she would have the courage to be honest. Then she wasn't sure how he'd react. She halted in midthought. Pastor Ray's kindly face rose in her mind. Could she find the courage to talk with him?

With the swell of the pipe organ, Kate bent down for the fifth time to adjust Phyllis's sweeping lace veil as she and Darren prepared for their triumphant recessional. Arm in arm, they headed down the aisle. Next in line, Kate stepped forward to follow, capturing Scott's arm. Her pulse raced.

Though she'd always considered Scott a handsome man, her heart somersaulted when she saw him in the afternoon, dressed in the black tuxedo that accentuated his broad shoulders and trim waist. He wore a lavender cummerbund and tie in a shade to match the attendants' dresses, and the pastel purple filled Kate's thoughts with spring—lilacs, creeping myrtle, grape hyacinth, and wild violets.

Clasping Scott's reassuring arm, Kate moved down the aisle, a smile on her face, her eyes seeking Amber. When she saw the girl's happy face, Kate gave a small wave, and the child lifted her hand and wiggled her fingers in greeting, wrenching Kate's love-filled heart. Scott and Amber. Together her life would be complete.

When she and Scott reached the foyer, they followed the bride and groom into the fellowship hall. Forming a receiving line, they greeted the guests, and when Amber arrived with Cass, Kate knelt and gave her a giant hug.

"You look pretty," Amber said, her eyes wide with excitement.

"Thanks. You look beautiful," Kate said in return, running her finger along the delicate trim of Amber's neckline.

With this being Amber's first wedding, Kate and

she had shopped for hours to find the perfect party dress almost the same shade as Kate's. Today, Kate had combed back the sides of Amber's hair and held it with a purple scrunch, the curls hanging like a ponytail of ringlets. Kate was a proud mother.

Amber stepped away and encircled Scott's neck with a giant squeeze, then skipped along with Cass, like a little lady. Kate's heart melted at the sight.

When the receiving line ended, Scott carried a stack of wedding cards across the room to Darren, and Kate hurried away to find Amber. The child was sipping a cup of frothy punch beside Cass at one of the round tables.

"Where's Scott?" Amber asked, as soon as Kate neared.

"Talking with Darren." Kate pointed a finger in their direction.

"Can I go?" Amber asked.

Kate gave her an agreeing nod, and she skipped off, her full-skirted tulle dress bouncing as she ran.

"Have a seat," Cass said, patting Amber's vacated chair.

Painfully aware of her tired feet, Kate thought the idea sounded good. She sat beside him with a relieved sigh.

"Punch?" he asked.

"Sure."

He rose and returned in a moment, bearing a glass filled with the fruity drink.

"Thanks." She took a sip. "Tastes good."

Cass leaned back in the chair, twirling his cup with an index finger. "You two surprise me."

"Amber and me?"

"No, you and Scott. He's crazy about you."

Crazy about you. "I know. But we're just good friends."

"Maybe, that's what *you* think, Kate, but that guy loves you. I thought you'd be engaged by now. I would have bet on it."

An uncomfortable flush edged up her neck. "Well, you're wrong."

Cass hesitated. "Don't tell me he hasn't asked you? I can't believe that." He arched a brow, as if waiting for an answer.

"He has, but—"

"Here you are," Scott said, halting her response.

Relieved, Kate rose. "Just giving my tired feet a break." She squeezed his arm. "I want to talk with Phyllis a minute, do you mind?"

"No, go ahead," Scott said. "I'll be right here when you get back."

Kate hurried off, thanking God Scott had interrupted the questions before Cass gave her the third degree. How could she explain?

Heading across the room, she noticed Pastor Ray talking with some wedding guests. *Pastor Ray.* An earlier thought struck her. While she struggled for courage, she couldn't stop now.

As he stepped away from the group, Kate nabbed his arm.

"Kate." He smiled.

"Could I ask you a favor?" Her voice sounded strained in her ears.

"Certainly." A puzzled expression leaped to his face. "Is something wrong?"

"No, well, yes, I suppose there is."

"Something here…today?" he asked.

"Oh, no, everything's lovely. It's a personal problem."

His face relaxed.

"I'd like to talk with you. That is, if you have time."

"Kate, I always have time for you. Did you mean now?"

"No, not today. Sunday? I know that's a bad day, but I've finally gotten courage, and I—" Tears pressed behind her eyes, and she struggled to gain control.

He touched her arm, his eyes insightful. "After service, Kate. If you're anxious to talk, I'm available." With the lump knotting in her throat, Kate only nodded.

"I'll see you tomorrow, then." He gave her arm a reassuring pat and moved away.

Kate hurried toward the rest room, her heart weighted with anguish, her mind clotted with fear.

With Amber tucked in bed, Kate slipped into a pair of slacks and a top, then joined Scott in the living room.

Stretched out on the sofa, he'd stripped the tie and cummerbund down to an open-necked shirt and trousers, his rented patent leather shoes tossed to the floor.

"You look comfy," Kate said.

"I am." He propped himself up on an elbow. "Tired?"

"A little, but my mind's still whirling. So don't worry about keeping me up, I need to unwind."

He patted the sofa beside him. "Come over here."

"Can't. You're hogging all the space."

He chuckled and slid his legs over the sofa and sat up. "No excuse now."

She rose and sat beside him. "Happy?"

"Sort of," he said.

Anticipating the direction of conversation, her heart hit a speed bump. She sent up a prayer that he not ask her anything serious tonight.

"You'd look beautiful in a white wedding dress, Kate."

White. She lowered her head without response.

"I'm sorry," he said. "I don't mean to push, but—"

"I know, Scott, you've waited a long time for an answer. I thought once my license came and Amber moved in that you'd be relieved."

He drew back, his face contorted with question. "Relieved?"

"I know you felt sorry for me that day when I was so stressed."

"I've never felt sorry for you, Kate. I've felt sorry for me."

"You?"

"Yes, because I love you so much...and you don't believe me."

Her stomach twisted into a tight knot, nausea rising to her throat. She swallowed, closing her eyes to subdue her emotions. "I don't feel very lovable."

"You've told me, Kate. I just don't understand why."

"Tomorrow." The word sailed off her tongue before she could halt it.

"What do you mean...tomorrow?"

The commitment was made...and maybe for the best. "We'll talk tomorrow." Her throat constricted. "I promise."

His eyes searched hers, a blend of relief and confusion filling his face. He nodded, then slipped his arms around her and pressed his cheek to hers.

Clinging to him, Kate felt the thud of his heart against her own. She loved Scott, and if God was willing, she would deal with her sin, then accept Scott's proposal. She wanted to be his wife with every fiber of her being.

As if God presented her a gift, the weight lifted from her heart. Tomorrow—the day she would say goodbye or embrace the love he offered.

Chapter Eighteen

Filled with nervous energy, Kate paced the living room, waiting for Scott to arrive from work.

The house seemed strange with Phyllis married and gone, but Amber's presence added a new challenge to her days. What had once been simple was now complex, like getting herself ready for work while getting Amber ready for school.

For Amber, the transition had presented its ups and downs. Though she had grown close to Kate during counseling, the child now faced a new school, a new home, and a new way of life. The loss of her grandmother and the dramatic change had dragged her nightmares out of hiding. But with prayer and love, they had faded to an occasional night of waking, before drifting back to sleep.

As Kate waited, she felt grateful and relieved that Amber was occupied for the evening. The occasion was her first sleep-over with her neighbor friend, Carrie. Now, in the impending silence, Kate heard every creak and groan of the rafters, every sound of traffic on the street.

She sank to the sofa and leaned her head against the cushion. Her mind reeled with her conversation earlier that day with Pastor Ray.

After they had prayed, Kate sat inside his office, the door closed, and wept uncontrollably admitting her sin and shame, revealing the presence of a daughter that she would never know, and telling him of Scott's love for her...and his belief in chastity.

Watching the pastor's face, Kate had feared seeing him blanch with her confession or hearing him mumble some patronizing words of forgiveness, then sending her out with a pat on the back.

Instead, his eyes were filled with compassion and his words were not his, but the Lord's. He reminded Kate of the biblical woman, deemed a sinner by the Pharisees, who had kissed and oiled Jesus' feet. Looking into her eyes, Pastor Ray spoke Jesus' words. "Your sins are forgiven."

In her heart, Kate knew God had forgiven her. The problem was she hadn't forgiven herself, and as the Lord's prayer reminded her, if she wanted to feel God's forgiveness fully, she had to forgive others, including herself.

The pastor's words washed over her. He had assured her that her sins were forgiven, the same as the woman in the Bible. "You've worshiped in the Lord's house each Sunday," Pastor Ray had told her, "you've given your time to HELP, you've taken a needy child into your home, and you've repented. In your own way, Kate, you've kissed Jesus' feet."

But Kate wondered. Had she really kissed Jesus' feet or were her actions an impossible attempt to buy forgiveness? She questioned herself. Could her deeds truly have been a reflection of her repentance?

When the conversation with Pastor Ray turned to Scott, Kate's heart had lifted. Trusting in the Lord's promise, her concern wasn't God's forgiveness, but Scott's. Then, the pastor reminded her that Scott demonstrated Christian virtues—compassion, kindness, humility, gentleness and patience—all the qualities that God commanded of His children. And if that were so…then Scott would also hear her confession and forgive her.

Thinking of the verse in Colossians, Kate was struck with the last sentence. "And over all these virtues put on love, which binds them all together in perfect unity." How could she deny that Scott had shown her love? He'd stuck by her side even though she pushed him away; he'd joined her search for answers about Amber's past, then embraced the girl as if she were his own; and he'd demonstrated his love for Kate in every thoughtful way.

"Forgive and put on love binding them as one." Kate wrapped the words around her heart. Was God directing her to bind herself to Scott in marriage? Did the words give her assurance of Scott's acceptance and pardon?

Recalling her past behavior, Kate realized she needed to ask Scott to forgive her for more than her sinful past. She needed forgiveness for her lack of trust and her unwillingness to accept his love.

With heightened anxiety, Kate rose and looked out the front window. She eyed her wristwatch. Six o'clock. Scott should be there any minute. Her head pounded, and she massaged her temples, hoping to ease the thunder in her ears.

Instead, she heard the slam of a car door, and her heart rose to her throat.

In a flash, Scott flung open the front door and called out a greeting.

Grasping her courage, Kate met him in the foyer.

He carried a small grocery bag in his arm. After giving her a fleeting kiss, Scott looked over her shoulder. "Where's the noisemaker?"

"Amber's spending the night with Carrie."

"On a school night?"

Though rattled by anxiety, she grinned. "You sound like her parent."

A ripple of good humor cured his lips, and he shrugged. "No school tomorrow?"

"Yes, there's school, but don't worry," she said, amazed at his concern. "Her class has a field trip early in the morning, so Carrie's mom offered to drive the girls to school.

"Where are they going?" Scott asked.

"The zoo. They're taking the first and second graders."

Scott glanced at the bag under his arm. "Then I

guess she'll have to wait for her ice cream. I bought her favorite. Double chocolate.''

''I'll put it in the freezer,'' Kate said, reaching for the bag. She struggled to remain calm and amiable, but their talk hung before her like a black curtain. They'd delayed it long enough. ''She'll enjoy it tomorrow.'' He placed the bag in her hand, then turned toward the kitchen.

Scott stopped her. ''Don't put the other flavors in. I'm ready for mine now.''

Her heart sank. ''Others?'' she asked.

''I bought your favorite. That goofy kind with the peanuts, marshmallow and cherries.''

He shot her a dazzling grin, and her heart melted as quickly as ice cream in the summer heat.

Mentally dealing with their delayed talk, Kate headed for the kitchen and Scott followed, watching while she dished up the dessert. Before she handed him the bowl, Scott slipped his arm around her waist and drew her to his side.

''I just want you to know that I think you're more luscious than that ice cream,'' he said.

Amazed, she stared at him. Had he totally forgotten her promise to talk with him? She tensed, and she knew he sensed it by the expression that shot across his face. She wanted to pull away, to escape the confines of his arms, to run outside so she could inhale the fresh air.

''Are you all right?'' he asked.

''Not really,'' she said, ''but it can wait.''

His quizzical expression changed to dismay, and the look punctured her heart.

"We should eat this before it melts," she said, hoping to veil her sharp words. "It looks good. Thanks."

"You're welcome," he mumbled.

Kate chastised herself. If she'd kept her emotions in check, the situation wouldn't have fallen apart. Now, Scott looked on edge and her anxiety heightened. "Let's go outside?"

Without answering, Scott stepped aside.

Kate moved ahead of him and hurried to the back door, then outside to a refreshing breeze.

He followed, and in unison, they crossed the lawn in silence and sank into the shaded glider.

Though the late spring flowers brightened the yard, Kate's thoughts faded the colors to blurry drab. Why didn't she trust God to guide her words and trust Scott to forgive her? Her weak faith frustrated her.

She ate the ice cream in half spoonfuls. The flavor was her favorite, and if she hadn't been so preoccupied, she would've hugged Scott for his thoughtfulness, much like Amber did with every gift she received.

But Kate's mind was nailed to her distress. She gave Scott a sidelong glance. As if he were alone, he kept his attention riveted to the dish of ice cream. The way she'd reacted, he might have been better off alone.

"I'm sorry, Scott. Very sorry. You brought the ice cream as a treat, and I acted terribly."

He didn't respond, but she knew he listened.

She continued. "It's not a good excuse, but my mind was tied up with our conversation last night. I'd promised to talk with you today, and—"

"That's why I brought the ice cream. A celebration."

Like cold, spiny fingers, regret worked up her spine. Unaware of the ensuing conversation, he'd planned a party. Her chest constricted around her hammering heart, and with shallowed gasps, she struggled to breathe. "I'm sorry," she said, the only words she could wrestled from her lips. "Maybe, I was wrong, Kate. I've been so certain that you'd trust me and tell me what's bothering you, then tell me that you love me. I was wrong."

"No, you're not wrong, Scott. I love you with all my heart. But I owe you an explanation."

A look of surprise jumped to his face. "Kate," he said, relief evident in his voice, "I've wanted you to trust me for so long." He captured her hand in his.

The confinement frightened her, and she slowly pulled her hand away, pressing it into her lap. "I talked with Pastor Ray this morning about us."

"About us? What about?" Scott asked, his voice constricted.

"About everything. Your proposal and my fears. He gave me a lot to think about and—

Scott straightened, shifted to the edge of the

glider, and faced her. "Kate, get on with it, please. I'm dangling over a cliff and I can't hang on much longer."

She had wanted to explain—lead up to her confession, but his complaint rankled her. "You want a bald-faced confession." She turned on him. "I'm not a virgin, Scott. I haven't been since I was fifteen."

His head jolted backward as if she'd slapped his face. Though his jaw dropped and moved like the gills of a fish out of water gasping for life, no words fell from his lips, no sound, only silence.

"I'm sorry. I've told you so often you deserve someone better than me. An untarnished Christian woman who'll love you the way you deserve."

"Kate…" Her name fell from his mouth in a breath.

"I know I've disappointed you. I've more than disappointed myself. I was young and stupid. That's not an excuse…it's a fact. I knew what I was doing, but I wanted to be popular and loved so badly that I didn't care. All my Christian upbringing went down the drain, along with my self-worth and hope."

Her voice trembled with each declaration, and tears pooled in her eyes and rolled unbidden down her face.

"Kate, please—"

"Don't stop me," she said and rattled on the hurt and shame she'd felt after she'd ruined her life.

"It's okay, Kate. I'm shocked but—"

"And that's not all, I had a baby daughter given for adoption when I was fifteen. She was born at…Madonna House." The last word faded into her sobs. She continued, "I'm unfit for a decent Christian man like you."

Scott reached out to hold her, but she pushed him away, sensing his shock, knowing he was repulsed.

Before she could stop herself, before she could catch her breath and realize what she'd done, Scott rose and stumbled away from her.

"I can't fight you any longer," he said. "This is the last thing I thought would happen tonight. I'm sorry, but I can't handle this." He spun on his heel and tore across the grass out of sight.

Kate curled into a ball on the glider, her body reeling with spasms of guilt, her sorrow knotted within her like a hangman's noose. She'd taken every measure of her inner bitterness and flung it at Scott as if he were the sinner, instead of her.

Forcing her tearstained eyes to open, Kate peered into the darkening heavens. The sunset bled across the sky in orange and scarlet, like fire and flames—like damnation.

Chapter Nineteen

During the night shift at County General, Scott's distraction concerned him. He struggled to concentrate on the patients and push his own desperation aside. He'd spent a couple of sleepless nights plodding through the horrible memory of Kate's disclosure, overwhelmed by the outcome.

Yet, her confession was the least devastating. What hurt him to the core was her lack of faith in him. After knowing him for a year, sharing untold hours together, why hadn't she told him sooner? He'd done everything under heaven to let her know that his life was empty without her, and still, she didn't trust him to share her doleful secret.

He thought back to her family's Christmas visit. The puzzling pieces fell into place, and the cheerless picture rose in his mind. Her Christian parents, so devastated by their daughter's offense, so fearful of gossip and disdain, shut her away in Madonna House, trying to do what they thought was right.

Scott's heart ached, envisioning the fifteen-year-old Kate, her slender frame bearing the swelling of her sin, alone and frightened. And he was sure she was as naive and vulnerable then as is a child. Scott imagined her parents' pain, wanting to be proud of their lovely young daughter, yet confronted by her disgrace. A family caught in the middle.

And...Kate's daughter. His chest tightened with the reality. A little girl, perhaps as lovely as Kate, was growing up somewhere in the vast United States, never knowing her birth mother. Thinking of his own situation, a mother he would never know, his personal longing yanked his emotions, and the old melancholy shrouded him.

Amber. Kate's tremendous longing took shape as he understood her desire to take the girl into her home. Though she could never atone for her own child, Scott saw how Kate might sense God was giving her a second chance.

The perplexing fragments of his relationship with Kate puddled in his mind. Scott moved from bed to bed, patient to patient, nailing his mind to their complaints and pushing his own aside until the shift ended and he drove home in a blur of bright sunlight and exhaustion.

With Cass on day shift, Scott had the condo to himself. He slipped off his shoes and made a cup of decaf. Bits of the past tumbled into his awareness and icy slivers of reality shredded his conscience.

Sitting right here in this room, he recalled a discussion with Cass and his prideful declaration. "Chastity is a precious gift between husband and wife." Those were his very words, and Kate was sitting in the room listening, her heart, most likely, aching with her own sorrow.

Scott flinched, remembering a day with Kate when he'd disclosed the situation with Lana. Again, he stressed his belief in chastity—how he'd stood up for his faith. And Kate sat beside him, defending him, telling him he was a real man. "Perfect" she'd said. And then, her final comment. "You listen to God and do what he asks. That's why you deserve the best."

Unbidden, tears flooded Scott's eyes, and his stomach cramped, holding back the deluge of emotion that washed over him. He never cried, not even over his humiliation with Lana, but today the misery poured from his heart and rolled down his cheeks. Kate meant more to him than a million Lanas. He hammered his fist against the sofa cushion, appalled that he'd been so stupid. So blind, not to understand sooner.

Kate, with her distorted perception, viewed herself as the worst, not the best for Scott. In her eyes, she was used goods, marred by her past. Yet, Scott perceived a different Kate—a lovely, ideal woman inside and out. A woman who cared about needy children, who gave her time to help others, who made him laugh…and made him cry, a woman who loved the Lord.

Somehow he had to show Kate she was wrong. Though he despised sin, he loved the sinner—a young girl who gave too much to be loved—so much that she no longer loved herself.

No one was without sin. Each person on earth allowed pride or money, career or lust, greed or gluttony—things that satisfy the flesh—destroy the spirit. Scott was a sinner.

A flash of memory cut through him the day Kate had told him her secret, and he'd let his pride respond, instead of compassion. Hurt that she'd pushed him away, irate that she'd kept her shame to herself for so long, he'd turned his back on her and walked away. That had been his gravest sin.

Why couldn't Kate see the truth? He cherished her. Determination rallied in him. He wouldn't give up, and in time, Kate would listen. She had to, because in Scott's eyes she was perfect. He loved her more than life and wanted her to know she was forgiven.

With Amber dancing around her legs, Kate put the last few items into the picnic basket.

"Are we ready, yet?" Amber asked for the hundredth time.

"When Phyllis and Darren get here. We're going with them."

Amber scurried out of the room, and Kate knew she was heading for the living room to press her nose against the picture window, to wait.

Her heart constricted. She had taken this little girl

into her life and heart, not realizing how few experiences she'd had. Living with her grandmother, a woman who probably struggled to make ends meet and whose energy level was different from a young mother's, certainly put a different spin on Amber's life. Picnics, amusement parks and travel were all unknowns in Amber's world.

Kate carried the basket to the living room and chuckled when Amber turned from the window to ask, "Is it time, yet?"

Repeating the same message that they were waiting for Phyllis and Darren, Kate kissed the girl's head and returned to the bedroom for just-in-case sweatshirts.

In her own room, she sat on the edge of the bed, clutching her shirt and overcome with loneliness. Scott had phoned three times during the past week, but she'd let the answering machine take the calls. She'd never been that unkind before, not even to salespeople, but she couldn't bear to be patronized or to hear another apology.

Yesterday, she received a bouquet of flowers, saying he loved her and asking to see her. She'd withdrawn the card and clutched it in her hand, her fingers trembling, wanting to call him so badly, but feeling that theirs was a love that could never be.

Only a week had passed since she saw him. It seemed like years. Kate had adjusted to her solitary life before Scott came along, but once she knew him, his absence left a hole as deep and wide as the Grand Canyon.

Even Amber questioned her. "Where's Scott?" she had asked. Not once a day, but numerous times, Amber's question stabbed through her. "Why doesn't Scott come to see us?"

Kate had used every excuse, except the truth. He's working, he's busy, he's away. The truth hurt more than the lies.

"They're here!" Amber's piping voice sailed into the bedroom.

Clutching the two sweatshirts, Kate rose and hurried to the living room. She hadn't seen Phyllis since she returned two days earlier from the honeymoon, and she was eager to hear about their romantic Caribbean cruise.

Kate pulled open the screen door and waved to Darren, standing by the trunk.

"Ready?" he asked.

She nodded and laughed as Amber darted through the doorway and scurried to the car with a Frisbee and ball clutched in her hands.

Kate grabbed the shirts, basket and her shoulder bag, then locked the door.

"Are we ready?" she echoed as she reached the car. "We've been ready since you called." She tilted her head indicating Amber, who'd already climbed into the car.

With their gear packed, Darren pulled out of the driveway, and from the moment Kate asked the question, the conversation was filled with the sights and sounds of their five-day cruise.

At the park, trying to keep her emotions in check,

Kate plastered a smile on her face, and whether playing Frisbee with an exuberant Amber or forcing herself to eat the picnic lunch, her heart wasn't in it.

After clearing away the paper dishes and storing the leftovers, Kate conceded to play blindman's bluff. When it was Kate's turn, Amber giggled so loudly that Kate could have found her in a flash. Instead, she held her hands in front of her, feeling the air, until she touched a muscled arm and, moving her hand upward, a man's jaw.

"Darren," she said laughing and pulling off her blindfold.

Kate's heart stopped. Scott stood in front of her, his face tired, his eyes serious.

"We need to talk, Kate. And you can't make a fuss."

Before Kate could respond, Amber was wrapped around his legs, bubbling with questions and nagging him to play.

He knelt down and gave her a bear hug. "I need to talk with Kate for a few minutes, okay? Then I promise I'll play whatever you want."

Though disappointed, Amber released his neck and stood aside while Scott captured Kate's arm.

"We'll only be a minute, Amber," Kate said, looking toward Phyllis and Darren and wondering if this picnic was part of a plot.

"We'll keep on eye on her," Phyllis called.

With Scott's arm linked to hers, Kate stretched her legs in long strides to keep up with him. He didn't speak, but she sensed his determination and knew that her protest wouldn't make a difference.

When they were out of sight of the others, Scott slowed. The sound of water floated on the air, and he guided her down a path to the stream. A large rock, like a granite bench, stood between the trees, and Scott stopped.

"Let's sit," he said, motioning to the huge stone.

"Phyllis told you we were coming here," Kate said, knowing the answer.

He nodded. "But Stoney Creek's a big park. I've been driving around for an hour looking for Darren's car."

"But why did—"

"I didn't know how else to corner you, Kate. I wasn't going to come to your house and stand outside while you refused to see me. That would confuse Amber and—"

"I understand," she said. "I haven't made it easy." Kate hesitated. But why had he dragged Phyllis into it? "What did you tell your sister, Scott? She acted the same as always, so she doesn't know about me. What did you tell her?"

He lowered his eyes. "I told her everything, Kate. I had to, so she'd understand what happened."

"But she's treated me—" Her senses spun with the awareness.

"Kate, the difficulty is yours. Yours alone. Phyllis felt only sorrow for what you went through all these years. She loves you like I do."

"You can't love me, Scott. That's why I didn't

answer the telephone. You might try to forgive my past, but you won't forget."

"There's nothing to forgive, Kate...and nothing to remember."

"But you walked out," she said, her heart rising to her throat. "When I told you, you said you couldn't handle it."

"I couldn't handle the fact that you didn't trust me enough to tell me sooner—that you pushed me away no matter what I did. That's what I couldn't handle, Kate. But I had time to think. I remembered so many things I said about chastity that must have torn you to the core."

The memory jolted her.

"I finally realized what I'd done. We can believe in something," he said. "We can know what God wants and try to do it, but we can't sit in judgment of others. We can't flaunt our Christianity as if our faith makes us better than someone else. That's being prideful—and that's what I did."

"No, you were standing up for your faith," Kate said, fighting the tears that pooled behind her eyes.

"You're being a social worker. From your gut, Kate, admit it. I hurt you so many times. I'm so sorry."

He slid his arms around her as moist droplets ran from his eyes and clung to his lashes. "Forgive me, please."

Her mind swirled with longing and fear. Could he ever forget? Then as if guided by God her mind filled with scripture. "Forgive as the Lord forgives you. And over all these virtues put on love, which binds them all together in perfect unity.''

"There's nothing to forgive," she said, her heart and arms yielding to his outpouring of love.

Scott stood and drew her from her rocky perch. With dewy eyes, he searched her face, and his voice nestled against her ear. "I love you, Kate. I have and always will.''

His lips neared hers, and without hesitation, Kate tilted her face upward, meeting his mouth.

Happiness and completeness rolled over her in waves of emotion. The strength of his arms, the masculine scent of his skin mingled with a spicy aftershave, the gentle touch of his powerful hands against her face, each enveloped her in a warm, safe comfort. The secrets of her heart were laid open and bare…and still, she was loved.

Scott drew back, his eyes glinting with the sunlight that filtered through the trees. "Let's do this right," he said, edging her backward toward the rock.

The granite pressed against her legs, and she sank to the hard seat. Scott clasped her hands with one of his and knelt against the sun-speckled earth. With the other hand, he reached into his pocket and withdrew a black velvet box.

Kate's heart soared. A nervous smile spread across her face.

"I've waited a long time to say this the right way." He looked into her eyes. "Will you be my wife, Kate? I want…" He faltered. "Even more… I need you and Amber to make my life complete."

Kate's heart swelled, pushing the joyful words from her lips. "Yes, yes, yes. I love you with all my heart." With tear-blurred vision, she gazed into his eyes. "I don't have to speak for Amber. You know she loves you."

He slipped the jeweler's box into her hand. When she lifted the lid, the sunshine reflected in the diamond and sent prisms of sparkling colors into the air, but not nearly so beautiful as the love glinting in Scott's eyes.

Chapter Twenty

Eleven Months Later

The stiff ruffled shirt pressed against Scott's Adam's apple, and he swallowed to control the engulfing emotion that pounded in his temples.

He looked down the aisle to the end of the white runner where Amber, in measured steps, concentrated on plucking pale-peach rose petals from a basket and dropping them along her path.

Her blond hair was swept into a cap of curls spilling over her crown where small white blossoms were tucked around the ringlets. Her pretty apricot-colored dress bounced below her knees as she headed toward him, an occasional shy smile flashing his way.

Filled with familial love, he looked at his parents dressed in their formal attire, their faces filled with pleasure and pride. Even Kate's parents had made the trip for the occasion, and across from his own folks, Kate's mother sat looking equally content.

At the front of the sanctuary, the bridal party waited, focusing on the end of the long runner. Phyllis and Darren standing nearby gave him a sidelong glance. Amazed, yet grateful, Scott looked at Kristin, Kate's matron of honor, a demure smile on her face. He thanked God that Kate's acceptance of his love had moved her to pardon her sister's flaws and to make amends in her own heart.

With the swell of the organ, the guests rose and turned toward the door. Scott caught his breath, seeing Kate on her father's arm walking toward him. Her ivory gown shimmered with sequins and beads, and a cascade of the same peach roses clustered with ivy and lace trailed down the folds of her gown.

Scott turned his eyes toward Amber, and seeing her loving grin riveted to Kate, he knew his world was complete.

Kate stared straight ahead down the long aisle. With trembling hands, she clung to her father's arm, washed in a sense of grateful forgiveness. Nothing was said, but her parent's arrival didn't knot her in fear as in the past. She welcomed them, bubbling with her own happiness, and she saw the change flow over into them.

With slow steps, they neared Scott who stood like a Titan, tall, strong and handsome. How many years would she have lived tangled in her own prison if

Scott hadn't given her the key to open the door of her heart?

Scott stepped forward, taking her arm, and Amber nestled at her side. Somewhere another young woman might be preparing to be a bride, a daughter Kate would never know, but today, with deeper understanding and familiarity with Scott's family, Kate was assured that God had guided her child to a loving home.

As they moved forward, Scott clasped her trembling hand in his. Feeling whole and cherished, Kate looked into Scott's love-filled eyes and listened as Pastor Ray read the joyful words, "Dearly beloved, we are gathered here in the presence of God and these witnesses to join this man and this woman in holy matrimony...."

* * * * *

If you enjoyed
SECRETS OF THE HEART,
you'll love Gail Martin's
exciting debut for
Silhouette Romance in:
HER SECRET LONGING
Available September 2001
Don't miss it!

Dear Reader,

Children's Haven is patterned after a real children's home in Oakland County. For many years I worked in the educational system as a licensed counselor, listening to individuals' heartaches, secret hurts and shames. As I wrote this story, I reflected on how we so often wish we could "rewind and erase" portions of our lives that cause us pain—incidents we wish we could hide and forget. But we cannot do that. Instead, like Kate, we bear the burden alone and allow our lives to be affected by the weight of our shame that depletes our trust, hope and spirit when we have a simple solution: give our sins and troubles to God.

I hope you enjoyed visiting with Kate and Scott, who with the Lord's help released their burdens and let Jesus carry their sorrow and shame. Then, following Jesus' command to "let the little children come," they opened their arms and hearts to little Amber. May God bless each of you as you trust and love one another during life's difficult moments, remembering that hope is an assurance when you trust in the Lord.

I appreciate and look forward to your comments and letters. Please look for my next Love Inspired novel.

Gail Gaymer Martin

Take 2 inspirational love stories FREE!

PLUS get a FREE surprise gift!

Special Limited-Time Offer

Mail to Steeple Hill Reader Service™

In U.S.	In Canada
3010 Walden Ave.	P.O. Box 609
P.O. Box 1867	Fort Erie, Ontario
Buffalo, NY 14240-1867	L2A 5X3

YES! Please send me 2 free Love Inspired® novels and my free surprise gift. After receiving them, if I don't wish to receive anymore, I can return the shipping statement marked cancel. If I don't cancel, I will receive 3 brand-new novels every month, before they're available in stores! Bill me at the low price of $3.74 each in the U.S. and $3.96 each in Canada, plus 25¢ shipping and handling and applicable sales tax, if any*. That's the complete price and a saving of over 10% off the cover prices—quite a bargain! I understand that accepting the books and gift places me under no obligation ever to buy any books. I can always return a shipment and cancel at any time. Even if I never buy another book from Steeple Hill, the 2 free books and the surprise gift are mine to keep forever.

103 IEN DFNX
303 IEN DFNW

Name	(PLEASE PRINT)	
Address	Apt. No.	
City	State/Prov.	Zip/Postal Code